Mental Ward:
STORIES FROM THE ASYLUM

Edited by Gloria Bobrowicz

Sirens Call Publications

Mental Ward:
Stories from the Asylum

Copyright © 2013 Sirens Call Publications
www.sirenscallpublications.com
Print Edition

Edited by Gloria Bobrowicz

Artwork © Dark Angel Photography
Cover Design © Sirens Call Publications

ISBN-13: 978-0615818795 (Sirens Call Publications)
ISBN-10: 061581879X

MENTAL WARD:
STORIES FROM THE ASYLUM

A CROWN FOR A RED QUEEN

Jennifer Loring

"Whatever ails you, Katherine, we shall find it and cure it."

The alienist's attendants slipped a jacket over Kate's head and her arms into the absurdly long sleeves. They folded her arms over her chest, then fastened the five straps tightly behind her, binding her arms into immobility. She did not resist. She hadn't the energy; not to eat or drink, dress or bathe herself, nor even to read her favorite books.

The ride out of the city and to the isolated island, linked only by a causeway that flooded with each tide, lasted at least two hours. Though the alienist and two attendants accompanied her as if she were a violent madwoman and not herself the victim of an unspeakable crime, Kate did not wish to be alone with her thoughts. She had trained herself to stay awake, and had not slept since that night a week ago.

But it wasn't enough. If her mind began to wander, she saw her sister in her blood-drenched dressing gown, her accusing eyes gleaming with the madness into which she had slipped before her death. Her hair had been plaited around her head, not yet taken down for bed. Her golden locks turned crimson, a crown for a red queen.

Kate twitched a little in the dingy white contraption that bound her. Her rear end ached from the hard, cold seat.

"Almost there, Katherine," the alienist reassured her in his kindly voice. But she knew better. Men were anything but kind.

***

Bloodworth Asylum looked every bit the part it was intended to play. This is why you pretend your mad relatives no longer exist, whispered the barred windows. The enormous iron gate shrieked like the damned when it opened, and barbed wire looped along the thick stone walls. And yet the perfect irony of the asylum's name was the only thing in a week that had brought a semblance of a smile to Kate's lips. *We shall find out,* she thought, *what my blood is worth indeed.*

Kate's arms had gone to sleep. Once the men escorted her into the mouth of madness and left her alone with the alienist, he removed her restraints and her arms flopped listlessly at her sides. She studied her new surroundings as he filled out an intake form. The ceilings and windows were very high, like a cathedral, the plastered white walls bare of any decoration that might put troubled minds at ease. Because, of course, those same decorations might set off other troubled minds.

"It is likely melancholia," said the alienist. "We will need to start treatment first thing in the morning." He pulled a gold pocket watch from his trousers. "Follow me, Miss Mayberry. I will show you to your bed."

As if she were in a fine hotel and not incarcerated in this dark, stale prison where the screaming never stopped, and in fact after a time became as normal as birdsong, or the train whistles blasting from the mainland across the otherwise silent channel. Pain was imprinted into the very atmosphere of the building. Were it empty Kate believed she could still hear the phantom screams.

4

Her bed, a crude cot with a shabby blanket and no pillow, lay within a large room in which similar beds lined the walls. Aside from the alienist and the attendants, there was not a man to be seen.

"Keep quiet," said the nurse, "and sleep. He will see you in the morning."

Few of the others were keeping quiet. Women and girls moaned and wept and shouted obscenities. Those not already restrained with either leather straps across their bodies or cuffs that trussed their wrists and ankles to the bed clawed at their dressing gowns or their own flesh. After a time a nurse or attendant came by with a dose of antimony that rendered them too nauseated to hurt themselves or anyone else, and strapped them down at the first opportunity.

"I do not sleep. I won't."

The nurse furrowed her brow. "Then I will have to administer a sedative and notify the alienist."

I should have said nothing. Just lain here until morning and pretended. But it was too late to recover her mistake. "Then do so. I will not go to sleep otherwise."

"And why not?"

Because she waits for me, Kate thought, but did not respond.

"Very well." The nurse produced a large syringe, already filled with liquid, from her pocket. She grasped Kate's arm with rough fingers and tapped the crook of her elbow, then jabbed the needle into a vein. Kate winced at the stick of sharp metal into her flesh. Her blood burbled up into the vial, replacing whatever poison now worked its way through her body. Kate pulled the blanket up over her head as sleep tugged at her eyelids.

I screamed, and no one came to my rescue. Do you remember?

Kate curled herself into a trembling ball. *Please, Sarah, please…what would you have me do?*

Her grasp on consciousness slipped away, and Kate tumbled headlong into a scarlet abyss.

***

Every quarter of an hour the sonorous chime of the oddly placed grandfather clocks in the sleeping room, the day room, and the hallway called out to Kate, even in the depths of her chemically-induced slumber. The alienist was there, gazing impatiently at his pocket watch. "Took your time, didn't you? No matter. You're the one they've been waiting for."

"Who? Waiting for what?"

"We have," said a choir of dreadful voices. The bodies to which they belonged remained unseen except for hazy, malformed shadows that bled into the darkness around them.

"I don't belong here." Kate turned to run, but all the walls had become mirrors, and in them dwelled her sister, who would reign forever in blood.

***

Some hours later a voice awakened Kate, if only because it simply would not stop talking. Kate dragged the blanket off her head. The girl next to her was not much older, and had been sent here after murdering her infant daughter.

"Remember," she whispered, in a tone suggesting a topic of utmost importance, "that six is afraid of seven, because seven eight nine."

Kate suppressed the urge to groan. "Why did you kill your child?"

The girl grinned. In the moonlight from the windows she appeared ghastly, all white skin and black eyes and rotting teeth. The sort of woman that fairy stories warned about, an evil hag who preyed on children.

"So they could never send her here," she said.

Kate tucked one arm under her head and stared up at the ceiling. The woman chuckled to herself.

"I beat them."

***

The first rays of dawn knocked feebly at the dusty glass when the nurse roused Kate from the depths of what had surely been a nightmare. Even now, tendrils of fear pricked at the corners of her mind, the dark spaces where Sarah made her home inside her sister. Wet, warm, bloody darkness.

With light creeping along the edges of the room like an intruder, Kate took stock of the room as her disorientation began to fade. Most of the women still slept. Some beds were empty.

"The alienist will see you now. Follow me."

Kate walked behind the nurse down a long hall, the stone floor cold against her bare feet. She passed the day room, unlit and empty at this hour. From other rooms whose doors were closed, she heard muffled voices and screams.

The nurse ushered her into a sterile white room bereft of any furnishings other than two chairs facing one another. The alienist already sat in one, a notepad perched upon his lap.

"Come in. Sit." He nodded to the nurse, who closed the door behind Kate. She took her seat.

"What…what did they tell you when they called you to our house?"

"That you had gone into a severely melancholic state upon your sister's self-murder and could not be roused from it."

"She didn't…I saw…"

He leaned forward. "Saw what, Katherine?"

"He did it. Raped her and slit her throat."

"And you did not try to stop it?"

"What could I do? He had a knife. And she was… She didn't want our parents to know…"

"That she was a whore. Do you feel guilty?"

What a stupid question, Kate thought. And then: *How did he know that about her?* "I loved her. Yet the man who killed her is still out there, and I'm locked up in here. Tell me who should feel guilty, doctor."

"Listen carefully, Katherine. It is my greatest desire to cure every girl in this hospital, but I expect full compliance. I will not abide disorder, of the mind or any other sort. You will find that those who do comply benefit from my kindness. My good girls take tea at six o'clock. You like tea, don't you?"

"I don't think—"

"Then you shouldn't talk."

The discourtesy of the comment stunned her into silence. She had been here less than a day, yet she already longed for the ordinary comfort of a cup of tea. She longed to be anywhere else, even home where Sarah most loved to

8

torment her, for Sarah drew power from the things she had so abruptly left behind. But it was strange, his manner of speaking, as if Kate had heard it before. As if she would not leave.

"Yes," she said, her voice barely audible to her own ears. "I like tea."

"Very good." The pocket watch appeared in his hand, despite the chiming of the clocks. "Forgive me, but I am late. Round goes the clock in a twinkling! The nurse will see you out."

***

Kate sat alone at a table in the day room. A large mirror, set in an ornate onyx frame and covered in fingerprints, hung on the wall beside her. An odd choice of frame. She wondered if there were people spying on the room from the other side.

Sarah's blood-streaked face grinned back at her.

"I'm Mary, by the way." The woman who had killed her child settled herself at the table.

"It wasn't very civil of you to sit down without being invited," Kate said.

Mary was unruffled. "As soon as I knew it was a girl, I started makin' my plan. I won't have them touchin' another one. Not from my family."

"What do you mean?" Kate lifted her head. Mary had just become infinitely more interesting.

"They look for the mad ones from poor families. The families who'll sell ya for a few shillings. It's money makes the world go round, don'tcha know. All so the men here can experiment on us."

"Experiment? I've seen no experiments here."

"Not yet, you haven't, but I have. They're experimentin' on us to make the perfect woman. Problem is, they take out so many of the human bits, what's left ain't a person at all. But I suppose that's what they're after, in the end. Somethin' that ain't human anymore."

I am in a madhouse. I should expect to hear mad things. "How do you know all this?"

"A while back I got friendly with one of the nurses. You get a good one, every now and then. She told me everything. This ain't even a real hospital. It's funded by a rich old bastard whose daughter ran off and ended up a whore in the streets. Next day wouldn't you know, they found the nurse dead. Said she killed herself, but they've got eyes everywhere in here. I know they did it."

"The mirrors?"

"Oh… the mirrors." A strange smile inched across Mary's face like a new breed of insect. She rose from the table and beckoned Kate to join her at the window. Several attendants scraped the broken remains of a woman off the lawn and dumped her into a sack. She must have got on the roof somehow and jumped. Another attendant splashed buckets of water on the grass to wash away the blood.

"They do it all the time. Or strangle themselves, or cut themselves. Whatever they can to escape, because no one wants to become a machine."

"A machine? What on earth…?"

"I know my time is runnin' out."

A nurse's shadow darkened the doorway before moving on. Mary scrunched up her dressing gown while the day room attendant was occupied with a woman who had decided to serenade the entire hospital with her rendition of "Twinkle Twinkle Little Star."

"Mary! Really!"

"They'll take me piece by piece."

"Mary, they can't… Dear God."

Brass gears dulled with blood, set inside a metal plate over her chest, whirred and clicked in a mechanical rhythm. "They said I had no heart, and so they took it."

"This is not happening." Kate stumbled away, but even as Mary dropped her gown and smoothed it over her knickers as if all was right with the world, Kate could hear nothing but the clockwork tick of the machine that kept Mary alive.

"Machines obey. Machines never shame their masters."

Kate flung chairs aside in her desperation to flee the day room. She skidded into the hallway, looking left and right for any nurses or attendants, but someone had shut off all the lights. She groped along the walls, and her fingers came away slick and smelling vaguely of damp metal.

Do you know what it feels like to bleed all the time? I'll bet they could show you. Drain it and pump it back in, forever. The blood flows in, the blood flows out…

Why are you doing this to me?" Kate cried, clutching at her hair with sticky fingers.

You should be ashamed of yourself.

"I went mad over what happened to you!"

Yes, that you did. It makes me smile. A smile as wide as the slit in my throat.

"What must I do to make you stop punishing me? What do you want?"

You must suffer. And now we shall have some fun.

The clocks chimed in unison, but the sound clanged through Kate's head as if the pendulums were striking her very skull. She crumpled to her knees, head gripped in her hands, and dry heaved. *Round goes the clock in a twinkling…*

"Tea time, ladies!"

Kate flattened herself against the wall. She cringed as the fluid seeped through her dressing gown, but it was the sight of the alienist striding toward her down the hall that made her pray she could turn invisible. He pushed a cart with a silver tea service on top into the day room. Candles burned on the tables, casting the grotesque silhouettes of misshapen children on the walls.

The cart clattered as it crossed the room. Kate took a step toward the direction of the front entrance, or at least where she thought she recalled it being, but disorientation had set upon her again. Nothing looked familiar; she was certain the walls were shifting and rearranging themselves.

A clammy hand shot out from the doorway. Kate screamed and clawed at it with her free hand, but it dragged her into the room, past the insane faces oblivious to her plight. The alienist threw her into a chair, and then began to pour tea and serve it with a cube of sugar to each of the patients. They chattered with high-pitched, unintelligible syllables like giant rodents in the language of the mad.

"Mary? Where is Mary?"

"Mary could not join us tonight. She has not been a good girl. But you like tea. You will be a good girl and drink your tea like a proper lady." He set a fluted china teacup before her. Kate stared down at the dark brown liquid. Something floated on the surface, or perhaps it was just a trick of the light.

Kate lifted the cup to her lips but hesitated before she drank. She looked around the room at the blank and waxy faces that eagerly gulped their tea as if no liquid had ever before quenched their thirst. Gears and clockwork whirred and ticked in place of absent organs. And everywhere Kate felt the cold glare of her sister, her pain and her rage and most of all her madness.

A coughing fit overcame one of the girls at the next table. The teacup slipped from her hand and shattered into tiny slivers, the tea itself dribbling down her chin like coal slag. It was so thick and dark, Kate realized, because it was mixed with blood.

Soon all the girls were coughing. They crawled about the floor and grasped at the china shards. The alienist's cadaverous face registered nothing but delight as he gleefully dipped his pocket watch into a full cup.

The girls slashed at their own wrists. Kate gazed down at the lattice of white scars inside both her wrists. Even when she'd tried, she hadn't the courage to go through with it, to feel even a fraction of the pain Sarah felt.

Kate leapt up from her chair and bolted for the hall. She slipped on a patch of blood and banged her hip against a table, but bit down on her lip to hold in her cry and hobbled onward toward the door.

"Katherine, come back! You've not had your tea!"

I have to find Mary. She must know what is happening.

Kate tiptoed along the slimy wall. The alienist might be following her, for all she knew, but nevertheless she rattled the knobs on locked doors, and peered into rooms from which no light emanated. Then, at last, she heard a soft sigh and ducked into the room from which it came. Another girl must have escaped the day room and found shelter here. Kate closed the door and felt along the wall for a sconce to turn on.

She wished she hadn't.

Mary lay strapped to a bed beneath four mechanical arms, naked and gleaming with metallic parts. If she so much as blinked, the machines whirred and prodded her with sharp instruments seeking to dig out anything organic. The infernal device that powered them, a pump of some sort, chugged in the corner.

"Little…star…" Mary croaked. One of the arms unleashed a metal claw that grasped her tongue and extended it as far as it would stretch. Another arm rotated, produced a pair of shears, and snipped the thick muscle clean off before depositing it in a glass container on a bedside tray. Kate covered her mouth lest she lose the dinner she could not remember eating.

"Nnn-kuh…Nnn-kuh…" said Mary, as blood gurgled in the back of her throat and spilled out from between her lips as if she'd just devoured someone.

There was no stopping it now. Kate turned away just as vomit forced its way between her fingers and onto the wall, the floor. She wiped her hand on her gown and doubled over until nothing, not even bile, remained in her stomach.

Kate scrambled out of the room, but the corridor had vanished. Mirrors haunted by Sarah's ruby specter replaced the walls, reflecting back on each other into infinity so that Kate could not determine where the hallway might turn left or right, if at all.

"Sarah, let me out! Please!"

A hundred, perhaps a thousand, of Sarahs' blood-rimmed eyes glared at her, boiling with all of a child's petulance and rage. She was too young to understand that Kate's fear had been as immediate and agonizing as Sarah's own, that it had paralyzed her, broken her. She felt as dead on the inside as Sarah was on the outside.

"I'm sorry! I'm sorry for everything!"

So am I. I have something to show you. Then, maybe, we will forgive one another.

Two of the mirrors scraped across the floor to reveal a doorway. Kate took a hesitant step inside; it was nothing more than a narrow walkway, which she followed until, several turns later, she was peering through a mirror that looked out onto what she thought should be the day room. But there was no day room anymore. A giant hedge maze now stood there, and Kate gazed into it from above as its denizens wandered aimlessly, ignorant of anyone or anything around them. Trapped within their individual nightmares they likely did not perceive a maze at all, but whatever terrors plagued their sick minds. *This is how they see themselves*, she thought. *Monstrous. Lost.* Kate pressed her hands against the mirror.

Mother sent us here last summer. Do you remember? We actually liked it here. We didn't want to come home, and I suppose a part of us never really left. We were safe here. Safe from the man selling us to his friends for extra money.

Kate shivered. She'd almost convinced herself that her father had not done those terrible things.

"You created all of this?"

From your pain. From the pain of all those who have come here. In life you had no control over anything, not even your own body. In death you can rule this world as its queen. They are trapped here, too, and so very desperate for someone to lead them from the maze.

15

"Death? What do you mean, 'in death?' I've no intention of dying here!"

A red light floated toward her from the depths of the corridor, and with it a coldness that rolled in like a storm front from the sea.

She ran. The darkness closed in around her, the red light so close behind her, closer…

But there was nowhere left to go, whether the wall was supposed to be there or Sarah had manipulated it into place as if operating her own personal chessboard. The futile pounding of Kate's fists thudded dully against the stone.

"Why machines, Sarah?"

Machines love unconditionally.

"Machines don't love. People do."

Father couldn't love.

The coldness crept up Kate's legs under her dressing gown, coiled around her insides and pierced into her heart. When she turned Sarah stood before her, bathed in her bloody light and drenched in gore the way she was a week ago, bleeding out on her own bed. The gash in her throat stretched and yawned.

You're a smart girl, Kate. It amuses me that you don't understand. Or refuse to.

"Understand…what?"

You never had a sister.

Kate shoved past the girl and darted into the pitch blackness of the passageway. Rats scurried ahead, warning of the intruder in their midst.

Why can you always hear me, Kate? Because I am inside your head. Because I am part of your own mind.

"I'm dreaming! I've always had bad dreams! I…"

You were so ashamed of what he'd done; selling you like a common whore for money he'd just drink away. He gave you a different name when you were working. He called you "Sarah," because deep down inside he could not live with himself if he thought of you as his daughter.

"I want to leave," Kate whispered.

I am your guilt, your shame, your anger. You gave me life. You wanted to punish yourself. Right now you are in a hospital clinging to life after slitting your own throat. You've fought valiantly for a week.

"Enough!"

Forgive yourself. Or reign here forever, made powerful by the dreams of the insane.

She stared down at her gown, the cotton a stiff and rusted red. Blood dribbled from her fingertips into the unseen crevasses between stones, and her feet were wet.

"I can help them."

And who will help you?

"I will take their pain. Their nightmares. I will let them know it's not their fault."

Perhaps one day you will turn that kindness toward yourself.

"Perhaps." Kate found the mirror again, or it may have appeared simply because she wished it, and gazed out at the world she had built for herself. Misery, suffering, the shared realm of the mad. When she looked behind her, Sarah was gone.

The walls dissolved, and Kate descended down a staircase into the labyrinth. The memory of her physical body broke apart and wafted away like smoke. The girl in the hospital had at last given up her fight.

You are safe here, she thought as she extended the tendrils of her mind into each wandering soul.

And you are mine.

WHISPERS

Alex Chase

"Please, tell me it won't hurt, doctor," Douglass looked at Doctor Harris with tear-filled eyes. Douglass was sitting in a plastic chair in a viewing room of the Eastburn Psychiatric Rehabilitation Facility. Doctor Harris was sitting across from him, separated by little more than empty air and a few feet of space.

The facility itself was fairly isolated. Set a few miles out from the nearest town, the location was far enough away that any escaped patient could easily be caught before reaching civilization. At the very least, those towns would be notified in time. A series of metal security gates, along with thick concrete walls, limited movement within and blocked cell phone communication entirely.

Doctor Harris was a plump man who was old enough for people to probe him about retirement plans, but not so old that they'd express surprise upon finding out that he was still employed. The pepper in his salt-and-pepper beard was the only thing protecting him from 'Santa Claus' jokes.

The doctor fought to appear objective; it wouldn't do any good to become emotional. It would be unprofessional and could result in the patient developing an unhealthy attachment to him. He forced himself to focus on the bland walls, the shining linoleum floors and the grate-covered windows as he launched into the same speech he'd given so many others in the past.

"Douglass, it won't hurt at all. You see, we give you a powerful anesthetic before the procedure. That way, you'll be unconscious. You'll lie there, sleeping peacefully while we use a controlled electrical…"

"I know what you'll do; I want to know that it won't hurt!" Douglass snapped. He doubled over, groaning and clutching at his head. "They're so loud," he whispered. "So loud, so angry. Voices like knives, like darkness, cutting at my soul."

Doctor Harris grimaced. This particular patient was afflicted with one of the most severe cases he had worked with. He was rarely violent, but there were four orderlies-two at each end of the room- just in case. The few times he'd physically reacted to something, it had proven nearly impossible to restrain him.

Douglass was a poor soul who was lost in a psychological void; he was too ill to live a normal life, but not ill enough to be blissfully mad. He'd heard about the Eastburn facility on the radio and wandered from town to town until he'd arrived at their doors, covered in rags, dirt and blood.

He was too detached from reality to give them a family history, though later discussions led Doctor Harris to believe his family was deceased. He didn't remember his own name ("Douglass" was a pseudonym) so they could not search for a social security number. His finger prints didn't turn up any records and his face was not matched to any existing driver's license. He could've been a ghost for all anyone knew about him. They'd taken him in out of pity, diverting finances from other departments to cover the cost of his stay.

Since being committed, he'd hesitantly admitted to being coerced into criminal activities by the 'black voice' and that the 'twisted one' convinced him that he wasn't wrong in doing so. During moments of clarity, he realized that what he'd done was unacceptable and attempted to resist the influence of the voices in his head. Eventually, though, he'd 'see the truth' and admit that 'they were right, because people really were trying to hurt him.' When confronted, he'd mutter that he had proof that no one else was allowed to see, then shut down and refuse to speak to anyone.

He acknowledged that he couldn't go on in his current state, so they had tried a number of therapeutic methods.

Doctor Harris had taken Douglass under his personal consideration, despite the fact that he had the entire facility to run. Incidentally, Doctor Harris was the only therapist Douglass would speak to. He communicated openly with the nursing staff, but trembled violently throughout any and all conversations with female members.

Doctor Harris has sat patiently through a variety of pharmacological therapies, knowing they wouldn't work on one such as Douglass. In building his practice, he'd done extensive reading and spoken with numerous others in the field, only to learn that patients who experienced cyclic lucidity were, in fact, harder to treat than the consistently psychotic. Unstable levels of serotonin and dopamine not only made finding the appropriate dosage nearly impossible; there had been a handful of cases where patients fatally overdosed. Doctor Harris had monitored Douglass closely, but, as he had expected, the patient did not improve.

They had attempted talk-based therapies only to learn that 'the voices' did not like the doctor's questioning techniques. While they seemed to ignore him during regular conversations, any psychoanalytic approach led to Douglass screaming in agony and writhing on the floor.

These fits were typically accompanied by saying that "he had to die" and other such threats.

After calming down, he'd weakly apologize for his behavior and beg the staff not to give up on him. They were only turning to electro-convulsive therapy as a last resort.

"It's ok, Douglass. We'll go through the procedure, and then hopefully the voices will be quiet, or quieter." The doctor did his best to reassure Douglass.

Still holding on to his head, Douglass nodded, tears streaming down his face. "Thank you."

Doctor Harris turned and nodded to an orderly. The man stepped forward, flanked by one male and one female nurse, and helped Douglass stand. The patient was very pale and weak from having skipped meals. More often than not, he'd scream, "I can't eat, I don't deserve to."

Douglass looked back, "You'll be there, won't you?"

Doctor Harris couldn't help but notice how youthful Douglass's face was; despite the dark eyes and frail smile, the man almost looked angelic. "Of course I will," he assured the patient, "I just need to arrange some paperwork. I'll be there shortly."

The doctor walked off as the staff took Douglass to the room designated for electro-convulsive therapy.

"Are you feeling ok today, Douglass?" the female nurse smiled at him, her blue eyes shimmering.

He looked strange, for a moment, like he couldn't decide what to say. He hurriedly said, "Yesthankyouhow'reyou?"

"Why, I'm fine, thank you, Douglass," she nodded politely. They had walked in silence for a few minutes when Douglass cleared his throat.

"You named me, didn't you? You're the one called me Douglass?"

She drew back. It wasn't unusual for the staff to talk about things and for the patients to overhear, but Douglass typically seemed too disconnected from reality to process what was going on around him. "Well, yes, actually. How did you know?"

He stared at her for a moment; their four sets of footsteps echoed through the hall like rolling waves of thunder. He could feel an avalanche building in his mind. He'd be buried if he didn't escape soon.

"A hunch." His answer was clipped, almost harsh.

They were at the door labeled ECT Therapy. "Are you ok?" She reached towards him.

Douglass jerked back, staring wide-eyed at her hand. She pulled it away. Douglass felt the orderly's fingers digging into his shoulder.

"I'm sorry," she said quietly, clutching her hand to her chest. He gulped nervously and tried to speak but couldn't. The two men directed him into the therapy room, where they laid him back on a table and began strapping him in.

There was a click and then Doctor Harris's voice filled the room. "We're going to secure you first and then we'll use a syringe to administer the anesthesia. You'll count backwards from ten, and when you're asleep, we'll begin the procedure. Is that ok?" The doctor was distorted by the static of the outdated intercom system making him sound like a robot. Listening to him made Douglass's skin crawl; he felt himself beginning to sweat.

He glanced at his restraints but decided it was too late to back out- besides, he did want to get better, and this would fix him, right?

"Yes, doctor." Douglass craned his neck and saw Doctor Harris watching him from the control room.

"Ok, good. Zack will administer the anesthesia now." The male nurse stepped forward and swabbed the crease of Douglass's left elbow with an alcohol pad. He then found a vein in Douglass's arm and stuck the needle into it.

Douglass felt the world too acutely. The leather of his restraints was like sandpaper grating away at his skin. Zack's syringe was like a dagger; for one terrifying moment, Douglass thought that the nurse was injecting a poison, but he forced himself not to believe that. It was a medication. It was going to put him to sleep. When he woke up, he'd be cured. He believed that. He had to.

"Count backwards from ten, please?" Zack's voice had the detached and passionless nature of someone who'd entered the medical world to make a difference and found himself powerless to do so. The words were frigid. They began to freeze the room. Douglass's saliva turned to ice inside his mouth.

He struggled to speak: "Ten... nine... eight... shev... sih... fff..." Douglass tried to continue but couldn't. He waited for sleep to overtake him. It didn't.

"He's out, doctor." Again, words like ice water, drip-drip-dripping from his pale lips. Icy lies, since he wasn't asleep.

Douglass tried to say that he was still awake. The words wouldn't form. He felt like he was suffocating but couldn't make himself breathe faster or deeper. He felt the leather against his arms and legs; he felt the ice-words trying to stop his brain. The nurses stepped forward to attach strange devices that beeped and hummed in time with his heart.

Worst of all, he felt himself trapped in his own head. He was alone with the voices now.

Looks like you aren't asleep, worm. They don't know that, though. Or are they pretending they don't? Maybe they just want to see the fear in your eyes.

If they're such professionals, they would've done their jobs correctly. They obviously didn't want to put you to sleep.

Obviously.

What are you going to do about this, insolent child? Hm?

"I… I don't… the doctor wouldn't harm me," he thought as the orderly clamped a large metal cage over his head and neck. It was pressing painfully into his face.

Trapped like the rat you are. Fitting.

Fitting would be if you placed that so-called doctor in this machine, see how he likes it. Better yet, if you drove him mad so he was condemned to live the life he forced on his 'patients.'

Not very original, Lilith, but I agree. Not that it matters. This moron wouldn't be able to pull off such a feat.

No child can accomplish anything without its parents, Samael. Isn't that right, beloved fool?

"No! I don't want you here anymore! I refuse to be subservient to your macabre intentions; I will never again allow myself to strike at those I love. I'll kill myself long before I kill another." He tried to scream but his throat wouldn't make words. The staff left the therapy room, shutting the door behind them. From the corner of his eye, Douglass saw them enter the control room.

Oh, looks like he doesn't want to kill anymore. Who do you think you're kidding? Murder is in your nature.

Such a stupid little creature. He doesn't even know himself. How does he think he'll get by without us? Does he really think we'll help him if he's so disobedient?

What do you propose we do with him, then?

"Nothing, you don't get to do anything with me! Sometimes you confuse me, but I'll be damned if I'm going to sit here and let you turn me into a marionette."

Then the therapy began. His vision seethed, turning bright blue as light exploded all around the room. He felt electricity tearing through his body; his muscles screamed as his heart slammed against his ribcage so hard that he was sure his ribs would break. The electricity cut off after a few seconds, but he felt violently ill. A tear rolled down his right cheek.

What's wrong? Don't you want to be 'better'?

No, no, I think he's just too weak. After all, he's alone in this world. No family left to love him, no friends to speak of… even the staff here is so sick of him that they'd rather see him dead!

How does that make you feel, boy? Does it upset you to know that you're alone?

Perhaps he simply prefers the solitude. He knows nobody could love him, so he doesn't even try. Poor little creature. I almost pity him, but there is no room in my heart for such weakness.

"I… do deserve love… this will fix me… I'll get rid of you… and get on with my life."

We're not going anywhere. Better get used to us.

If you accepted us as a part of you, maybe we'd feel a little less ambivalent about helping you, but you treat us so disrespectfully…

The voices hushed as a second round of electricity coursed through him. A white-hot fire pounded through his veins. For a few seconds, his vision faded to black. He prayed that sleep or death would come to him. His prayers went unanswered. His body continued to shake uncontrollably.

"I… I know… it's working… you don't talk… while it's…"

You really think a few volts of electricity are going to stop us?

What do you take us for? Do you think we're as pathetic and weak as you? Do you think we're some daydream that is going to fade away when you leave? We are so much more than you can ever know. You should consider it an honor to be our puppet.

Worthless imbecile. You'd be crawling through the muck of your so-called society without us.

Vile wretch. You have no home in this world or the next.

We can get you out of here. Make you into someone significant.

We can save your life, not that you have one to save.

If you cooperate, so will we.

If you accommodate our requests, we would be happy to do the same.

Acknowledge us and together we will flourish.

Accept us, and the world is yours.

"No… I…" His thoughts were sluggish and weak. Between the voltage passing through his head and the voices trying to tear him apart from the inside, he wasn't sure how much longer he could fight.

Round three was stronger than the others. He felt a stabbing sensation as the electricity branded his brain. The surge felt like it tore open his skin and exposed him to the world. He imagined the nurse would be looking into his soul itself, if this continued.

He also couldn't remember his time in middle school. The doctor did warn him about memory loss.

Look at that, it's starting to eat away at your memories.

This machine is taking away who you are, little one. You're lucky there's only one shock left.

"How… do you… know…?"

We know everything. We know all about you, your potentials, your life… we know when and how you're going to die. But don't ask. The fun is in not knowing.

We also know it's only a matter of time before you give in.

We want to help you, but you refuse. Do you remember your own name? We know it. Do you know how to escape this place? We do. Do you want to live? We can grant you life again.

We're your ticket out of this hell hole. Even if you could get rid of us- which you can't- they'll never let you leave. They'll say, "You need monitoring, just in case" but try to give you the same medication that clouded your mind and stole your thoughts away.

What do you say, child? Are we friends?

The final surge hit him like a freight train- or it would have, if he could figure out what a train was. He saw blackness, then violent, bloody images. Giants in suits crushing villages beneath steel-toed boots. Children feasting on their parents to survive. Blank-eyed men who stared vacantly at a false world that imploded in on itself, formed and collapsed again- a thirty-minute lifespan that was trapped in a loop. He tasted blood. He was damp with sweat. Through it all, he heard the screaming of all the lost souls of a thousand burning cities filling his ears.

He lay there, unthinking, as the staff entered the room. The orderly removed his restraints as the nurses checked his vital signs. He was then put on a gurney and steered towards his sleeping quarters.

As he passed by the control room, he heard Doctor Harris say, "I highly doubt that this will cause any improvement in his condition. It should sedate behavior and alleviate depression... but don't expect significant results."

Your answer?

His head was spinning, both from the electricity and from what he'd heard. The doctor had no faith in the treatment? Then why put him through it? Unless...

"Can you believe we're still trying to help this guy?" The orderly said to the male nurse.

"Think we should spike his food with a little extra medicine? Kick him over the edge?"

"Nah, too traceable. Pills don't just go missing."

They were planning to kill him! He'd accused Lilith of just stirring up trouble when she'd suggested that a few days earlier. He didn't want to believe it, but he didn't have that luxury now.

"…you were right," he thought. "You were right all along… so yes. Friends."

The orderly brought him to his room where he was thrown casually onto his bed. The door creaked as it was shut; he heard the lock clicking into place.

Excellent. I'm proud to see that you've grown up a bit.

I'm glad you've come around to see things our way.

We're going to have some fun, Hugh.

"Is that my name?" he thought groggily.

Yes. Don't worry about that now, though. Rest. You'll need it.

His eyes drifted shut of their own accord. He was asleep seconds later. His sleep was deep, dreamless and undisturbed until he woke up eleven hours later.

He awoke to the sound of rain against his window. Sitting up, he stared through the metal grating and out through the glass beyond. Thick clouds blocked out the sun. The scene was so dark that the street lamps had stayed on, even though his wall clock- which was inside a small cage- showed that it was half past eight.

Good morning, Hugh.

You seem to have slept well.

Hugh was surprised to feel a smile creeping over his face. "Good morning to you both," he whispered. It was sort of nice to have "friends."

His bed was little more than a cot that had been bolted to the floor. He'd been given one sheet and one pillow, though it had been made clear that any attempt to harm himself or someone else would result in them being revoked. A meal had been pushed through the flap at the bottom of his door. It appeared to be some sort of egg dish, but he couldn't tell what it was. He rarely ate eggs.

He heard his stomach grumble.

I wouldn't go near that if I were you.

You heard the men talking. They were plotting. Scheming. They wanted to hurt you. They could've tampered with this food.

Hugh nodded. "I understand." He shoved the plate through the flap in the door, food untouched.

I'm very happy to hear that you consider us to be your friends, Hugh. Those are called scrambled eggs, by the way.

Hugh nodded thoughtfully, feeling the emptiness of his stomach.

Today's agenda: find clothes, break out of this place, get as far away as we can. Do as little collateral damage as possible.

The black voice, apparently called Samael, had a more militant personality than Hugh. It was comforting. Hugh remembered little about his childhood, but he distinctly remembered being messy and easily pushed around. The black voice wouldn't allow that. It also made sure he disposed of any evidence when he committed a crime.

No collateral damage? Where's the fun in simply walking away? I want blood, guys. The twisted one, Lilith, had always been like that. She'd encouraged him to torment his victims and laughed gleefully through the entire process. Her moods were infectious; what she felt, she made Hugh feel too.

Because of this, he killed over a dozen people in three different states. Samael made sure there was no evidence or repetition of killing methods, so the authorities had no way to trace him or connect the 'isolated' incidents. Lilith traded the wanton violence for emotional support. She would build him up on the corpses of his victims, but if he didn't slake her bloodlust, she'd tear him apart.

The staff had no idea who they were dealing with. All he'd told them was about burglaries and an arson case when he was 16.

"I'll see what I can do to satisfy you both, ok?"

Satisfy us? Why us? You're the one that wants to see this place burn. We're not the ones who were tortured and ridiculed. YOU want to kill Doctor Harris.

"I… no I… do I?" He couldn't deny the anger he was holding in his heart.

The doctor lied to you. He said he'd help you, but he only made you suffer.

"Did he lie?" He found himself breathing heavily; he was furious at how he'd been treated.

He said we'd be quiet if you went through ECT. Are we? Can you still hear us?

"Well… yes…" He couldn't deny her logic.

Then are you man enough to admit that you're pissed?

"Fine, yes, I am," he growled.

Good. Shall we?

"…Shall we what?" He cocked his head.

Leave. Just knock and you'll be able to get out of this room. They haven't checked on you yet. They'll want to see how you're doing.

Hugh shrugged, stood up and knocked. He heard footsteps from beyond; the lock clicked open and a different orderly opened the door.

"Good morning, Douglass," the man smiled. Hugh nodded.

He jerked forward, smashing the orderly's nose with his forehead. The man stumbled back and Hugh brought his leg up, kicking him in the jaw. He grabbed the falling man and pitched him back into his own cell. No one was around to notice.

"You were right, again," Hugh whispered, grinning.

See? You're enjoying yourself.

Hugh pressed his fingers to his lips, feeling the upward curve. He hadn't smiled in so long that the sensation was almost painful. "I guess so… where's Doctor Harris?"

Lock the orderly in your cell. Go to the dayroom. They spoke in unison.

Hugh took care to hide the body beneath his bed. He grabbed the key ring and baton off the orderly's belt, tucking both into the waistband of his underwear. His oversized patient's shirt hid the weapon well.

He shut the door and made sure to lock it. All personal rooms were kept locked when empty so that others couldn't hide inside them, meaning that no one would care that his own door was shut tight.

Hugh walked into the dayroom, which was used as the group therapy area, leisure activity area and medicine distribution area, though not at the same time. Doctor Harris was easy to spot among the shambling people he referred to as 'patients.'

The thinly-clothed patients wandered around with no intention or desire. They were dead or dying. Their flesh already rotting... only able to move because their minds hadn't realized they'd passed on. Hugh nearly choked on the stench of decay.

The doctor, however, had giant, reflective eyes and greasy, slicked back hair. His flesh seemed ready to peel away and reveal the snake beneath.

Walk up to him as if everything's normal. Hugh did so.

"Hello Douglass!" The doctor seemed alarmed. "I'm surprised you're out of bed so early. Most spend quite some time in bed, resting after such a procedure."

Repeat: I couldn't help it, I was too excited.

"I couldn't help it, I was too excited," Hugh beamed.

There are no more voices in my head.

"There are no more voices in my head."

The doctor looked as though he'd been struck. "Are-are you sure?"

How couldn't I be?

It would be pretty hard to get 'voices' and 'no voices' mixed up.

"How couldn't I be? It would be pretty hard to get 'voices' and 'no voices' mixed up." Hugh smirked; this was too easy.

"My, my, I'm very glad to see the progress that you've made..." the doctor tapped his chin thoughtfully. "I'd like to place you on a low-level dose of anti-psychotic medication, just to prevent the risk of relapse."

"So when would I be able to leave?" Hugh knew what the answer would be, but had to ask.

"I'm afraid you'll have to remain with us for a few months more. You need monitoring, just in case."

Told you. He has no intention of letting you go.

He is a charlatan who profits from madness. This facility is subsidized. He gets paid by the patient, not the hour. Don't listen to his greedy lies.

"I'd prefer I not take the medication, if that's ok," Hugh shuffled his feet. "It makes me feel like my head is stuck in a swamp."

"I insist, Douglass. It's the best thing we can do for you right now."

Careful… the foxiest men are also the most cowardly… you cannot kill what is hiding in its den…

"Can we talk first? Like, really talk? One-on-one?" Hugh said eagerly. "They never let me talk to you like that before. Maybe it'll prove that I'm fine now."

Doctor Harris smiled, "Why, that's an excellent idea. Joyce," he turned to a woman nearby. "I'm going to speak with Douglass in my office."

The woman nodded as Hugh followed the doctor to his office. It was a posh, well-furnished room that reflected the decade-and-a-half he'd spent in the halls of Ivy League schools. The volumes of psychological theory upon his shelves were caked with dust. Doctor Harris shut the door, taking a seat behind his desk.

"So, since this is your first real session of talk therapy, where would you like to start?"

Maybe we could discuss my father. I hated him.

"Maybe we could talk about my pops, you know? I hated the man. Right up until the day he died." Hugh leaned back in his chair, completely at ease with what was happening.

The doctor leaned forward, "I'm sorry to hear that. What happened to him, if you don't mind my asking?"

"I spiked his morning Corona with a bit of anti-freeze. Did you know that just four drops can take down a two-hundred and fifty pound man?"

The doctor blanched, his eyes wide.

How sickeningly unprofessional of him… Now let's talk about the way he put you through ECT, even though he expected it to fail.

"You know, doc, I don't appreciate that you put me through shock therapy when you were so sure it wouldn't work. I thought we were buddies, doc. Friends. Pals. But you're another god damn snake, rolling around in the money pits, acting like people like me are just rats for you to get fat off of." Hugh kept his eyes locked on the doctor, who began to tremble.

"What do you mean?" The man sputtered.

"I heard you," he hissed. "I was awake the whole damn time."

"What- that… I…" the doctor was aghast.

"Don't bother. A lie for a lie, right?" Hugh grinned.

The doctor was becoming notably pale. "I don't understand what you mean, Douglass."

Now.

Hugh drew the baton from his waist and brought it cracking down along the doctor's jaw, shattering it. He fell from the chair as Hugh darted up, locking the door. He heard an orderly knock.

The doctor lay on the floor, in too much agony to scream, as he tried to crawl away from his assailant

"You lied when you said it would help. I lied when I said I was cured." He felt a grin split his face. He could feel an excited wildness fill him; he saw colors more clearly, heard things more distinctly, he could even swear he smelled the fear coming off of Doctor Harris. "Don't worry, I won't kill you… I've got a better idea in mind." He slammed the baton against the doctor's left knee, breaking it. There was no way the aged man was going to escape.

He keeps a vial of Sodium Pentothal in his refrigerator.

Ram that needle into his neck. Make him bleed into his throat and drown in his own blood. A quick death is far too kind for this swine.

Hugh walked over and drew a syringe full of the liquid. The knocking grew more urgent. Hugh stepped over and opened the door.

He glanced back. "By the way, my name is Hugh."

An orderly stepped in but Hugh rammed the needle into the man's neck before he could speak. Gurgling softly, he collapsed. Hugh refilled the needle and shut the door quietly behind him, noticing the blood oozing from the man's mouth.

The voices spoke to him for a moment. His eyes widened. "Oh, that's a good idea!" He walked to the right, heading towards the main security post.

The staff was currently changing shifts. The only people left were the few still in the stations. Lilith and

Samael kept him well informed of where the cameras were and where they were facing. No one could've seen him coming.

Hugh rounded one corner, then another and finally came across the main station, which had two doors- one behind the entry gate and one in front. You'd have to pass by the window to leave.

Hugh, however, had the keys.

He put his hand on the doorknob, unlocking it. He tightened his grip on the baton.

Open the door; turn one quarter to the left, swing diagonally.

Bash his skull in!

He shoved open the door, turned and struck. The guard collapsed. That frenzied excitement came back, stronger than before. A heat began to fill him. It made him dizzy. It made him feel powerful.

Kill him. Kill him. Kill him. Kill him. Kill him. Kill him. Lilith began chanting steadily.

"Which control is it? What am I doing here?" Hugh shook his head, trying to focus.

Pull levers-

Kill him kill him kill him kill him kill him kill him kill him kill him kill him kill him-

"No, I'm not-"

Levers-

KILL HIM KILL HIM-

Hugh's breath came in ragged gasps. The world was spinning and shifting before him. The walls were melting and the sky was burning. All he could see was an explosion of red light and the man lying on the ground.

Damn it, Lil-

KILL KILL KILL KILL KILL KILL KILL KILL KILL KILL KILL

Hugh brought the baton over his head and slammed it down through the guard's eye socket, not noticing as blood exploded out from around the weapon and all over his face. The guard's blood cleansed his world, returning it to normal. The fire was gone and the walls were back. He was safe.

Standing over the desecrated remains of the facility guard, Hugh noticed a euphoria spreading through him. He stumbled over to lock the door he'd come through before collapsing into a fit of spasmodic laughter. There was something savage, some primal glee that assured him that death really was the key to living.

See, wasn't that fun? Oh, by the way, search his front left shirt pocket.

"What?" Hugh sputtered through bursts of laughter. He reached forward, fumbling around in the pocket and pulling out a scrap of paper, torn from some larger sheet. He was still smiling wildly.

Scrawled in barely legible handwriting were the words: Turn off camera 6 at 8:25. Douglass is a lost cause; we're not wasting any more time on him. -DNH

"Who.. Conspiring to kill me?" Hugh stopped laughing.

DNH- Doctor Neil Harris. You see, ninety-nine percent of the human race doesn't deserve to live and there's no way to tell who falls in that one remaining percent. They can't be trusted. You can't allow people to live if they're just going to hurt you.

"If they…" He was finding it difficult to argue. It all made too much sense. He began experiencing the dizzying sensation of an epiphany.

When someone kills a person who is trying to kill them, it's ok, because it's self-defense. This man was helping others to kill you. Therefore, it's ok. You shouldn't be mourning or feeling guilty. You should be celebrating.

"But… The doctor?"

The ringleader of it all. They were all in on it. It's not like there's anyone left to mourn you. They figured they could get away with it. You're making the right decision. Finish the job. Make them bleed. Make them suffer in this life, just in case they don't get an afterlife.

Ah, the old 'kill others to make sure you stay on top' trick- survival of the fittest at its finest. I'm usually in favor of not dirtying one's hands, but to each his or her own. Now let's get a move on.

Hugh nodded, rage replacing remorse as his eyes narrowed to become beady slits. "Which levers?"

One, two, four and seven, then punch the override button on the left.

He pulled those levers and smacked his hand down on a small red button. He watched the iron grates in front of him clang down. Glancing at the camera, he saw gates open all throughout the Eastburn facility- but the staff would be trapped in the west wing with the violent offenders and court-mandated patients.

All of the patient rooms had all automatically opened when he hit the override switch. It also disabled the building's phone lines.

Hugh blocked the door he'd come through with a chair before casually walking out through the other. He pushed open the front doors and felt the sun hit his face. He looked up, smiling.

He turned back for a moment, looking down the hallway. "Doc... My one regret is not being able to watch as your own patients tear you apart, piece by piece, before the whole lot of you starve to death."

He let the door slam shut behind him.

THE DOCTOR'S SESSION

Russell Linton

You followed her home, unable to contain the excitement. As she entered her house, you pretended not to notice and sidled along the street whistling a made up tune that sounded fantastic. Professional even, like you were a composer or artist. And you were. The thoughts made you giddy and high in that moment, the one before what would come next. It was always that way. You kept walking and smiled bright and big at the wonderful surprises the future held.

You saw her again, the very next day, as she left the laundromat with a green mesh bag slung over her narrow shoulders. She was there every Tuesday, while you drank your coffee at the shop across the street, watching her pass by through the steam in your cup.

Sometimes, she would look. Her dark eyes darting with urgent hops or scrunched in thought about the things on the edge of her senses. That told you she knew. The secret had floated to her on the insubstantial drift of heat you peered through. A secret whispered only to the chosen. You shivered, with delight.

That August day in the rain - her hair clung to her soft, round cheeks. Her skin was prepared and made pale and cool by a gray world. You thought for sure that was *the* time. The moment where she would become. She would transcend. She would fulfill the fevered whispers.

You pushed open the gate, left unlatched and ajar, the excitement of invitation rushing through your veins. Red and bright was the door, so bright! It glowed in the cloud scattered haze. It spoke to you of the beautiful future trapped within. It wanted to be released. She wanted to help you.

But as you closed your hand tightly on the brass handle, the surface still warm from the clutch of her delicate fingers, the latch would not give. You were uninvited.

No, no, not today, impatient little boy. Gathering your pieces, your scattered remnants, you stepped away from the door. Your blood returned from places unclean. Patience and time were all you needed. You just didn't know how much that was going to be.

***

CONFIDENTIAL

PSYCHOLOGICAL EVALUATION

Name: XXXXXXXXXXXXX

Age: 25 years, 9 months

Tests Given:
Thematic Apperception Test (TAT)
Brown ADD Scales
Wechsler Adult Intelligence Scale- Third Edition (WAIS-III)
Minnesota Multiphasic Personality Inventory MMPI
Substance Abuse Subtle Screening Inventory (SASSI)
Bender-Gestalt Test of Visual-Motor Integration (BGVMT)
Beck Depression Inventory (BDI)

Brief Psychiatric Rating Scale (BPRS)

REASON FOR REFERRAL
Patient was apprehended two weeks ago by local police officers for suspicion of murder and is awaiting trial. Defense attorneys have requested a full psychological evaluation to determine mental competency of said patient pursuant to Florida Statute Title XLVII 916.12.

BACKGROUND INFORMATION
Patient states that he believes himself to be in excellent physical health. Patient reports infrequent periods of 'black-outs' and being unable to recall portions of his day. He explains these black-outs have been occurring since the age of fourteen. Such black-outs have contributed to a few socially awkward incidents and minor injuries, but never, to his knowledge anything 'serious'. At times, the incidents are preceded by voices which have urged him to commit irrational acts. To the best of his knowledge, he has resisted the horrific instruction of these voices.

Developmental/Family: Patient states that he grew up in a traditional household with a father, mother and two sisters. Both parents were deeply religious, devout in their faith and required church attendance three times per week. He reports that his parents ultimately had marital problems which led to him taking a strong role in the family and the care of his sisters. He believes these difficult circumstances to have matured him and made him the caring man he is today.

Health/Medical: Patient describes the black-outs and voices to be the work of the Devil. When he was fifteen, his parents took him to a priest to have an exorcism performed. This, the patient believes, helped stabilize his condition. Because of his faith, he believed a psychological diagnosis to be unnecessary.

BEHAVIORAL OBSERVATIONS
The patient exhibited nervous demeanor and concern over his predicament. He was well-groomed but expressed discomfort about having to wear the clothing provided by the correctional facility. The patient appeared to be attentive to all tasks presented to him and aware and oriented to his surroundings. Exhibited a preoccupation with religious imagery and made frequent references to his faith. Reported concerns that the Devil had in fact won a battle over his soul; despite this, circumstances are believed to have led to useful interpretive data on all tests.

ASSESSMENT RESULTS AND IMPRESSIONS
Cognitive Functioning: Results of the WAIS-III indicate patient has cognitive ability that falls well above the normal range. Verbal and nonverbal measurements fall within the 96th percentile. Tests indicate strong ability with social convention and abstract concepts. High average scores were indicated for memory skills with extremely strong visual recognition.

Patient appeared hyper-focused when given tasks. When not presented with tasks, patient appeared nervous and wary of surroundings. During these intervals, patient on occasion described hearing voices. Self-reporting measures did not indicate any level of Attention Deficit Disorder.

SOCIAL/EMOTIONAL: Standardized assessments were performed during which patient was alert and focused. Answers indicate strongly toward a diagnosis of Paranoid Schizophrenia.

SUMMARY and RECOMMENDATIONS
Reviewer recommends patient be admitted into psychiatric care for further evaluation. Patient should be made more comfortable by providing him with casual clothing while at the institution. The patient has enormous potential to be a productive member of society given his cognitive abilities. A treatment plan including regular counseling and psychotropic medications is recommended to lessen the effect of the patient's hallucinations and delusions.

***

Clean up! Clean up! Now it's time for clean up! Clean up! Clean up! Or the basement you will go!

Stupid. Stupid. Stupid.

You curse your idiocy. You were in a hurry, so many weeks ago. Weeks before you came to know the red door. You did not clean up properly.

They saw the secret and it wasn't for them. Then they came for you. Dragged you away with handcuffs - on you!

They gave you an attorney and took you to a courthouse, back and forth. Back and forth! They want to kill you, but they're weak. They don't understand the meaning behind things. They can't and won't ever be able to wrap their pitiful minds around it.

They want to play games. That makes all secrets fun, but they don't even understand how to do that right. Days pass and it's all about talking. They just need to act. You know this.

It's calling again, but you can't leave. The red door, different from the boring off-white door before you. Off-white door, concrete floor, brain numbing white. White. Bleached bone. Whore.

Fine. You'll play their games.

There is so much time now. No one to complain about the noise, or the smell. There are free books that you can study to help tie their rules into twisty knots that dig deep into flesh. Some of the books are at the jail. Others, you ask the attorney to bring. He *must* help you. You are discovering yourself you tell him. Trying to understand why you did the horrible things. These are books that tell you the way to win the game. Law, psychology - you memorize every pertinent detail.

You finally leave the prison for a new place. A transfer to a new kind of cell. There are no more bars, except on the windows - windows so deep you can't reach the glass. You are taken to an office by a man with a bullfrog throat and iron hands. He tells you to sit. Across from you is a woman in a white coat.

She wears a cross around her neck. Her eyes look at you, directly at you. The badge on her shirt says Doctor Cynthia Morella. Her function must be to heal things, so the beauty of the broken is lost to her. She is pointless, like the rest. She asks so many stupid questions. Questions you answer like the books told you to.

The frames on the wall contain the story of her life. Her undergraduate diploma is in theology from a Baptist University, but her remaining education is in medicine and psychology, both earned at private religious institutions. There is a picture of a man and a young child on her desk. Yellowed with age and set into the oval of a metal frame. He watches the camera with a furrowed brow and clenched lips. She is a blur in a darkened gown that is banded around the arms and flares out at each shoulder. Her face is a streak of shadow and deep lines except for the white-hot spot of a reflected flash or damaged film just where her mouth should be.

You tell Doctor Morella about your family in ways she will understand. You mimic her eyes and the faces she makes. You cry. You tell her about your parent's religion and how they loved God and forgave and sang hymns. You tell her how you held together your family in times of trouble. You are a healer too.

Oh, how you have so much in common with Doctor Morella, don't you?

Truth and lies - the best way to speak to those that want to steal your secrets. You tell about the priest that came and prayed over you. The attempt to scare away the Devil. Hah! The Devil! Nothing controls you or makes you do the things you want!

Things you don't mention from when you were a child. Your only friends, found along Route 364. Crushed and ripped open to the sky and left for you to breathe life back into their insect-ridden forms.

You simply tell her the priest came to fix the black-outs. Black-outs like the one which made you hurt someone. Some one. Only one. You only ever hurt one, it's true.

She leans close, closer than any dare. The cross hangs crooked from the chain. Feverish breath warms you and her eyes flicker to almost a solid onyx before you blink and you see they are not different. The fluorescent lights buzzing above you must have winked out for that second. People's eyes never pierce you like that. It makes a flutter in your chest. You look away.

Then she demands more about the things the priest said and did. You give her the truth about those meaningless things.

You take tests. They ask some of the same questions over and over, using different words. You memorize your answers and make them match. The ones that fit the brain that won't be allowed to talk at the courthouse are the ones you pick.

Medicine. You tell them God has forbidden it, but that only keeps them at bay for so long. Finally you agree. You tell them you want to get better. You take the pills, swish with the cup and let them think you swallowed. They look, but cannot tell. You are special.

The best of your secrets save you from their poison. No one can poison you. The musty stench of soiled underwear clamped across your face. The cotton fuzz drawing out the moisture of your tongue and her face above you, *Don't you gag! Don't you make a mess on my floor!*

No. No messes. You control your every tiny muscle and flap of flesh within your throat. There is no mess and the things that go in can be drawn back and hidden. Hidden as long as you want.

It's not like the chosen who you share your secrets with. They wretch and vomit and you wallow in their weakness.

You let the doctors think the pills are gone. You speak to them politely, nimbly skirting by the things they aren't worthy of hearing. You remember what the books said, the ones in prison and the ones your attorney brought.

The books also told you to keep nervous and anxious about the voices. It isn't hard. You hear them scream, deep in your mind, in that special place where the most valued treasures are buried. Only now, you have to pretend you hear them aloud. You call them the Devil, so the Doctors will believe. So that Morella will blame Him. You can tell she understands, completely.

The books also told you to eat seconds and thirds at meal times. They monitor the food you get, so you trade for more. Getting what you need from the people here is so easy. All of them - stupid, crazy. And they think YOU need to be here. It makes you angry. You hear the pulse of the Red Door.

Weeks pass. You do not return to the courtroom. You must be winning.

***

Handwritten Session Notes
Doctor Rufus Connely

1:15 pm
The patient is on time for the session without prompting by staff. Patient inquires about Doctor Morella. Informed patient she is attending to personal business and will see him later in the week.
Discussed patient milestones in treatment. So far, all metrics satisfied and has shown swift reaction to medication with minor side effects. Patient complains about moderate weight gain - attribute to medication.

Milk
Tilapia
Wine - Pinot Grigio

Patient is cooperative. Fills out self-assessment survey for treatment goals.

5:00pm tee time - contact Dr. Sharp and Allen

Call wife, Gartner on invite?

Patient reports Charles Umbridge from C wing has offered him medications. Reports Mr. Umbridge may have extra meds - will have staff investigate.

Responses quick, intelligible. Conversational. Grooming +

***

You have been here a long time. Longer than the closet with the lock on the outside. Longer than the reeking confines of the bolted dumpster. Longer than the darkness of the basement, even. They don't understand how patient Mother made you. How much waiting makes things even better. Almost a year. You have never waited so deliciously long.

The last of the chosen, you waited for three months. Three months before you were invited to share your secrets. She walked by every day. By the coffee shop, through the steam. She never stopped and heard the whispers. But the day you brought them to her, she knew.

Up the stairs, feeling the echoes of her skin on the rail. To the door. This door was dull and green and opened with the slightest touch.

Shower running, tiny screams, teeth in your palm, the syringe fell to the slippery floor and shattered. Eight it took to get it perfect! Eight! Eight before you learned the way to make them all rigid with nothing moving but their eyes. It was so much easier then to show them the secrets, out among the trees and friends by the rural route.

But this one refused to learn the way you wanted so you changed the rules, for her.

Teeth biting deep into your palm, your hand entwined with clumps of hair, you slid to the sweating floor. Your hands met the tile, hard. She stopped. Soon, black blood reached out from a shining pool and the sharp corners between the tiles filled in tiny streams.

You gave her the secrets right there. You showered above her sunken eyes. Then you took her away to a different place because she didn't deserve to be with the others.

So many distractions. So many changes. It made you feel the clean up was done, when you weren't even started. Stupid!

They found the bone, matched the teeth - yours and hers. That will never happen again. Next time it will be like the first. And the time after that. And the third and fourth.

You lick your lips. Once for each time.

On the fifty first, the red door hums and throbs.

Calling.

Calling.

Soon.

You say it out loud and the words make you shiver even as you clasp your hand tight across your mouth. Could they hear? You see the dull door and its tiny window; empty glass with only wire mesh peering in. The clean and sharp corners of the walls, rising up, up out of reach. A single chair slices a corner in two, dark brown fabric with narrow trim, like veins close to the surface.

You have been here so long. No one has ever heard you. You whisper secrets into the emptiness and shudder in delight.

***

From: Dr. Jonathan Durand
<jon.durand@westboro.org>
To: Dr. Cynthia Morella
<morella.cynthia@westboro.org>
Subject: Re. Final Recommendations Patient 34276A

Are we one hundred percent positive on this recommendation? Due to the graphic nature of the case, we need to be certain. The media has stopped calling but the family of the victim has been continuing to press the DA for criminal prosecution. Safety of the community and the patient should be our utmost concern.

You wrote:
For thirteen months, XXXXXXXXXXXXX has been undergoing extensive psychiatric evaluation and rehabilitation. He is responding very well to pharmaceutical treatments and his hallucinatory episodes have been brought under control. There have been no known episodes in the past seven months. He has adopted a more stable view regarding his religious beliefs and recognizes the importance of maintaining psychiatric care.

Through continued counseling and medication, it is the opinion of myself and the medical staff at the Westboro Institute, that XXXXXXXXXXXXX be emancipated from state custody and transferred to a community facility where he can be provided supervision while he reintegrates into society."

Jonathan Durand, M.D.
Westboro Institute
Department of Psychiatry
2355 S. Maple Lane
Rexburg, VA

Office: 857-465-2001
After-Hours: 869-572-8679

***

From:Cynthia Morella
<morella.cynthia@westboro.org>
To: Dr. Jonathan Durand
<jon.durand@westboro.org>
Subject: Re. Re. Final Recommendations Patient
34276A

Myself and, of course, Doctor Connely, feel certain this is the right move. I have faith in the patient's recovery and strongly support our diagnosis. Personal faith not only as a licensed and learned psychiatrist specializing in the needs of such extreme cases, but also a deeper faith and understanding in a God which I share with the patient in question. This man is ready to return to his life.

Yes, the details of the case were extreme, but it has no bearing on his current mental state. Now that he has accepted and realizes the value of proper treatment, he will be able to stay on the right path and hopefully be open to continued contact with our staff when the need arises.

As far as the media, we're running a mental rehabilitation unit, not a public relations campaign. Give them the standard confidentiality statements if they start asking questions.

Have a blessed night,

Cynthia Morella, M.D.
Westboro Institute
Department of Psychiatry
2355 S. Maple Lane

Rexburg, VA
Office: 857-465-2007
After-Hours: 857-492-5468

***

You gulp down the coffee and let it burn your tongue and sear your throat. They did not serve coffee at the institution. Caffeine made the morons unmanageable. You were never unmanageable. Polite and responsive says the report tucked in your pocket. "Under control" it says. You smile. You order more coffee.

In the mornings and the late nights and the deep in-betweens when you would speak your secrets to the empty room, you thought of this special place: your seat at the window where you could speak to the chosen. You could watch the laundromat where so many of them came to wash their things. All sorts of wonderful things - pink with lace and tiny bows, black as old bruises and razor thin, fresh white bands taut like sinew.

After a year, will she still be here? Will someone else be your chosen?

You take a sip of your fresh coffee and through the undulating curtain of steam, you see her. It's not the raven haired girl with delicate hands and slender shoulders, her skin still glistening with an August rain. It's someone else. Someone you could never have expected. Doctor Morella.

She carries a blue basket balanced on her hip. A layer of clothing peeks through the barred gaps. Your fingers burn as you grip the cup and she disappears into the laundromat.

There is no need to whisper *anything*.

By the time you touch the cup to your lips again, the coffee is stale and cold. Your hands sting with a pain that has sunk into the marrow of your fingers. She is leaving the laundromat, her basket in hand. You wash down the tepid bitterness left in the cup and it reignites in your belly. You stride to the door.

Doctor Morella walks down the street, the basket banging against her side. Soupy air enters your lungs in short, ragged breaths. You follow from the opposite sidewalk, afraid she will hear your hammering heart. But she never turns.

She walks.

Walking.

Walking.

The pulse throbs.

Throbbing.

Throbbing.

She turns and disappears. Behind the red door. You do not hesitate.

***

The brass latch sinks like a knife through dead flesh and the door swings open effortlessly.

At last, you are invited in.

Chest drumming with a rhythm that courses through your neck, you close the door while scanning what lies within.

A short hallway and expanse of darkly grained wood flowing into the living room beyond.

Creme colored walls and antique trim.

A fireplace burning against the wall opposite the door.

Chameleon-like, the deep brown leather chair rising from the floor.

There is nothing else.

No one else.

The door behind you is white and pristine.

You step forward.

Closed, unlocked, the whiteness of the door behind is marred by your dancing shadow.

Moving forward into the living room, you run your hand along the arm of the chair. Yes, she is here, somewhere. In the darkness of the adjoining rooms perhaps. The chair, melting into the brown of the wooden floor, you know that you can be invisible here, too. You can sit, and speak the secrets, and she'll never hear. She'll never hear until it's time for you to show her.

As you lean back, the fire flares and wavers. You conjure forth the dead, resurrecting them with your breath. Each in turn, fifty utterances. More than simple names, they are an invocation. They are a power you alone can summon.

The shadows in the room take flight and a murder of dark shapes swirls cyclonic around you. Some reach out, some convulse or even grasp at insubstantial throats as they wail in misery. Each struggling form in its turn assails your brain in vivid, glorious detail. Samantha with the dying eyes that saw her own body, lifeless below her, her mouth moving as if to call out for it to follow. Nicole who lay limp and thrashing, her eyes rolled back to watch the knife wiggle in her skull. Taquesha, lovely Taquesha, so radiant on the inside in the fading evening light. A palette of crimson, mauve and the glistening white of cartilage and bone. So many more. The thoughts quickly excite you.

As the parade of the chosen comes to a close, you see a new shape that flows among them. Doctor Morella's naked form flickers in frozen moments between the writhing umbra as you stare. She stops and examines each form, so close you think they can feel her hot breath like you felt, that day in her office, when she asked about the priest. You want her to reach out and touch them. You want her to feel the power and the presence that only you can create. But in the swirling maelstrom, she passes between them with tantalizing closeness.

Morella's form jerks swiftly on the periphery, slipping into depths of deep shadow which you cannot penetrate.

In the filth of the dumpster, the locked closet, the frigid basement; always you could see.

From out of the black she stalks on hands and knees, slithering up your legs, her bare breasts rubbing against your shins and resting soft upon your knees. She is naked and her true self is bared to you.

Ebon talons wind their way up your thighs from long slender fingers. An unblinking and bottomless glare burrows through you broken by tendrils of smoke which rise from her lips. A burning heat in her mouth glows translucent through her cheeks. As she speaks, you feel the wash of hot words, trailed by charcoal wisps.

"You would play a game? With me?"

"What are you?"

She slides up your chest and you see the cross, dangling from her neck. It burns red hot and is reflected on her skin in a blistered outline of curling skin and charred bone. She watches your eyes with a curious twist of her mouth.

"I wear it to remind me of exactly what I am."

Your eyes go to the door which glows in the darkness of the hallway. The twist of her mouth splays open and jagged teeth draw forth as the hidden fire sparks inside an ivory cage. You reach your hand into your pocket and feel for the syringe. Full of the toxins and chemicals you use on your chosen.

You struggle to speak, "But... what is that? What are you?"

"A collector. Like you."

Your hand shakes in the recesses of your pocket as you fumble with the cap. Her eyes never leave yours, but the empty stare knows. You can tell she knows your every thought. She presses closer, her nose brushing the static field of your own, yet never touching. Tantalizingly close. The heat from her mouth singes your lips and you gasp as a cloud of pungent smoke forces its way down your throat.

"Do it," she hisses.

You start to slide the syringe from your pocket. The needle catches on the edge and it tumbles from your grasp. At first you wonder if it has impaled your leg in the fall, for your body ignores your pleas. Searching for the syringe, clawing your way past her, fleeing, it is all futile. You can only stare into her bottomless eyes. She lunges forward and you close your eyes, wincing, your face scrunched with the horrible anticipation you have seen in so many. A jet of fluid scalds your face. Your eyes spring open with your screams and you see her toothed tongue retracting into a molten furnace.

She grasps your head and forces it back, digging the points of her talon shrouded fingers into your scalp. "This is your duty, your purpose! Do not test me, do not fail me! You will give me what I seek or you have no need to continue here. Give me what I seek, or I shall render you unto them." With a vicious jerk she slips to the side and wags your head roughly toward the swirling shades.

Instantly, their screams subside and the darkness grows around you. Deep, deep, deeper than the clouded midnight spent beneath the shed. Its touch is eager and all encompassing and Morella watches it creep up your body like a passing cloud. Everything beyond it - your feet, your ankles, now your calves and knees, is hungrily devoured. Morella cackles and draws back, perching on the arm of the chair with a wild grin. Her breathing rattles with restless nerves as she shrinks away.

Everywhere it touches, there is nothing. No pain, no pleasure, no hot, not cold. Nothing but the emptiness.

"No! No! Make it stop! Anything you want! Anything!"

Morella leans forward with a hiss, sparks showering the chaos. The hungry night floods backward and away while you wait to see your body return from beneath its cloak. She releases your scalp and drops to the floor, her head resting on the arm of the chair. An incongruous look of child-like longing crosses her features as she tilts her cheek against the leather. Her hand burrows between the cushions, tearing them away until it emerges with the syringe balanced delicately between her claws.

"Do it like you did for them."

***

Handwritten Session Notes
Doctor Rufus Connely

Assumed case after extended leave of absence by Dr. Morella.

8:00 AM Continuing follow-up treatment with XXXXXXXXXXXXXX. Patient voluntarily admitted self into care after less than a week on release. Symptoms of serious relapse of Schizophrenia and psychosis are evident. Patient presented with first degree burns to right cheek. Restrained by staff on three occasions, each time calling for Doctor Cynthia Morella.

Verify Morella's emergency contact list, again

Sessions currently performed in patient's room. Patient is unstable, babbles incoherently and broke three restraining devices at regular "lights out". Sedated 6...

Deep gash of pen ink

...7 times. Recommend movement to high security ward. Four point restraints and sedation as necessary for the immediate future.

Move tee time to 4:00 pm
Call club, let them know we'll be dining afterwards
Reserve best bottle of whatever they've got. It's been a hell of a week!

HIERARCHY

Joseph A. Pinto

I have learned a great deal in my time trapped here. If only the others could say the same...

If only these walls could speak.

But Gloria does. Incessantly. And has not stopped since first admitted to this ward. *Ward.* I cannot help but snicker at my Freudian slip. The word, cold and unforgiving in its own right, nonetheless suggests the tiniest sliver of hope when spoken in my mind. But cold and unforgiving would be a welcome reprieve for the hell these husks of wasting flesh find themselves trapped within; nothing more than common livestock to be herded, slowly quartered. I will recognize it for what it truly is, then—an *asylum*, alive of its own accord, its sickened heart bloated with the poison coursing through this decrepit place.

Since first wheeled on the gurney through these doors, Gloria has not shut up.

Chattering to invisible entities —friends, family, perhaps? Always, no one is there; of this, I am quite sure. No soul, living or dead, aspires to linger within this rotted canyon of the lost. Gloria does not truly speak, however; she mouths unintelligible, disconnected exhalations that one would assume are sentences. In truth, they are nothing more than neurotic blatherings. I am sure Gloria did not ask for this. No sane person would. Still, she finds herself here, like so many of the others, the corners of her lips moist with drool, soiled rag of what passes as a nightgown hanging about her emaciated body. Aside from the haunts in her mind, she remains alone. Still, I possess no pity for her.

Not for any of them.

Today, Gloria sits before a crooked wooden desk, a tepid bowl of tomato soup atop its warped surface. She shoves a rusted spoon and a single piece of moldy white bread to the side. Into the coagulating surface of the soup she dips her hand, and then proceeds to greedily suck upon her slickened fingers. The sound simply unbearable, is still a welcome reprieve from her babbling. She slurps each finger down to the knuckle until the bowl is half consumed. Face and gown now a pink slathered mess, she slumps forward.

Then she talks to the walls.

She rambles, a mad incantation of mangled syllables, every so often chortling over her stream of nonsense. Every so often she nods, some sense of approval discovered within the conversation polluting her brain. Today, however, something is different. I have listened to her ravings with as much patience as one could expect, tirelessly enduring as the sun rises and falls beyond the bars of her grime-stained window. Now her endless torrent of gibberish ceases. Now something coherent comes forth from her lips. *"I... hear..."*

Anxiously I await more, but her focus shifts from the shadows of nether that only her cloudy eyes seem to pinpoint to the orderly that shuffles through the doorway.

A puzzled look upon his greasy face slowly fades as he scans her room for the sound. He has little to check over—sparse, generic furniture squats upon the squalid floors. Characterless, colorless. Lifeless, like so much here. He blows a disgusted sigh from his pudgy cheeks. "You're a mess."

Gloria reaches for her white bread. Nibbles disinterestedly on a broken corner of crust.

"You're worse than a baby. I'd rather clean a shitty diaper instead of you." He looms over her. "I should leave you like this. Slob."

She pecks at the opposite corner, a tiny, nervous bird. Crumbs sprinkle the pink stains of her gown.

"I said I should leave you like this," he persists.

She stares at her lap and continues to chew, trapped in the shadow of the orderly.

Finally he moves, dragging his feet to the small bathroom just a few feet away. He pulls a cold, damp washcloth from a crooked rack, wrinkles his nose. "This place sucks," he mutters, pinching the washcloth between two fingers as if sodden with the plague itself. He hates the asylum, but we all know he has no other opportunity for employment. He lacks the brains, the drive, to fit in anywhere else. Here, he remains as much a mindless zombie as the rest of the lot.

"Take it." His shadow looms over Gloria again, washcloth dangling before her face. She takes another bite of white bread, her lower jaw working it over as though cud in her mouth. He has always lacked the patience, and compassion, for this part of his job. "Take it," he demands, but Gloria does not answer. I must admit, his insistence humors me. *A slow-study, indeed.*

The orderly shakes the washcloth, face reddening with each passing second. "Take the fucking rag." He clutches at a frail wrist, jerking it into the air. Gloria gasps; with shock or in pain, I am not sure. But I silently continue to observe, my own curiosity heightening in tune with the ire of the orderly

He wrenches her arm over her head, lifting her body from the chair. The orderly does not know his own strength; Arnold has always been a brutish man, something I could not quite understand. Why exhibit your force over the weak, the feeble, when to break the spirit of the strong is so much more empowering? But Arnold prefers the meek, it seems. He squeezes upon Gloria's wrist, her cheeks now the color of her soup from strain.

Teeth clenching, his words tear through his heaving breath: "Take the fucking *rag!*" Fingers wriggle within his meaty paw, and her bare feet slap the grimy floor. Yet Gloria does nothing; she does not acknowledge Arnold, nor does she reach for the filthy cloth. He whips her then, the washcloth snapping from the air into her face, the suddenness of the act more vicious than the impact itself. She blinks, confused, the washcloth glancing off her pink-crusted chin, mouth sucking wind like a desperate fish. Arnold cocks his arm once more; he strikes across the bridge of her nose, and this time the washcloth leaves an angry welt. His eyes widen with shameless excitement.

It is absurd, a flogging by washcloth, but each blow falls with more purpose than the last, and soon her pain becomes a palpable, awkwardly delicious thing. I almost feel ashamed savoring her distress—almost. I have been on the receiving end of punishment countless times, yet this tang, so pungent, so distinct above the considerable raunch of urine and feces that cloys the sour air, becomes something new to my senses each time. So I observe... washcloth a ridiculous blur through the air... Gloria's face now a swollen lump. She does not shield herself; somehow, the white bread remains in her clasp.

Arnold grunts in disgust, chest heaving with effort. He tosses the dirty cloth to the floor, Gloria's arm still held captive above her head. "Filthy piece of shit," brow wrinkling, scrutinizing his handiwork. "You're going to learn not to make such a mess. Hear me? I ain't your goddamn mother." One swipe and he sends the bowl of soup flipping over the desk; it shatters across the floor in pink shards. He torques further upon her wrist, lifting her fully from the chair. She groans, eyes hollow, searching for the nether. Drawing his twisted face into her own, he hisses again, "I ain't your goddamn mother."

He shakes her like a doll, the chair spilling beneath her, and his face explodes with rage. Relinquishing his grasp, he circles her, a rabid animal, neck tense, nostrils widening. It is all I can do to keep myself from laughing over his posturing, but I am familiar with Arnold and this is his way. He peers through the doorway into the hall, so shameful in its silence. It is as though the residents of the asylum know what is coming, and perhaps they do. None dare step from their rooms. There is a system in place here, and we must all do our part. We allow what will pass to pass. We allow what is to be... to be. Such is the creed of the asylum. I was forced to learn the order; so shall Gloria.

With ferocity, he descends upon her. By the scruff of the neck, he seizes her, slams her face first into the wall. Spittle flies from her mouth, those cloudy eyes of hers vacant, eyelids fluttering. He kicks her legs apart. Licks his lips. Fumbles with his pants. *Oh, Arnold... always preying on the weak.* Frantically, he hikes her gown over her legs.

"I... hear..."

He freezes and slowly eases his grip. "What?" Part confusion, part incredulity. It is the first time he has heard her utter words.

Gloria remains cheek to wall. Tears bleed into flaked, crusted paint. *"I... I..."*

I wish I could urge her to go on. But she will, in her own good time.

Arnold smacks her in the back of her head.

"I... I..."

Brow glistening with beads of sweat, he smacks her again. "What the fuck you babbling about?"

I certainly get it. But Arnold does not.

"I... hear... I hear them all..."

Her visible eye roams within its socket, reveling in the nether. Then it stops. Widens. From her mouth rips something between maniacal giggling and a hysterical screech.

***

If only these walls could speak.

It is what Thomas mutters nearly every God-given day. Within this asylum, God has come to die, and crucifixion would seem a blissful, peaceful passing to what this place has in store. Thomas has been incarcerated for nearly as long as Gloria, though their paths hardly cross. Mind you, this is not exactly the truth. Their paths cross almost daily, but inside their deteriorated minds, they have assumed the identity of someone, or something else. Strangers on the most intimate of levels. It is the easiest way to sustain yourself here in the asylum. Sustain and little else, for there is no hope to survive.

Thomas speaks with clarity. The walls have never answered him, yet he continues aloud. "Got to walk the dog today. Chilly morn, though. Where's that sweater?

You seen my sweater? My dog needs it. Got to walk the dog today. You know dogs can't piss if they're cold."

The orderly points to a yellowed newspaper at the foot of Thomas's bed. "Right there. In front of you all the while."

Thomas seems surprised. "Well hol-ee Christ, there it is, right in front of me all the while. You should've said so sooner. Now where the hell is my damn dog at?"

The orderly smiles, hands Thomas a small white cup. He offers multicolored pills from an open palm. No one questions what the pills are or where they came from. Not the orderly. Not Thomas. Certainly not me. Thomas grabs them. He never takes the water accompanying his pills. It would make things much easier, but why he refuses, who knows. "Not drinking this water," Thomas says and swallows without flinching. Smacks his lips in satisfaction. I am certain he cannot taste a thing. "Now where the hell is my damn dog at?"

Benny shakes his head. "Damn fool. You don't have no dog."

A tragic thing, really.   Since Thomas was first wheeled into this asylum upon the gurney, he has called out for his dog. Eyes forever rolling within the misshapen skull of his, as if searching the countryside for his best friend. Have you ever noticed that upon closer inspection, eyes always speak of untold stories? I often wonder if his four-legged companion, real or imagined, still waits in never-ending fields of fancy.

"My dog... course I got my dog. She's all I have. She never walks without her sweater when the morns are cold. You know she can't piss if she's cold."

Benny stoops, whispers into Thomas' ear. "Your dog gone and died, Mr. Thomas."

I know what comes next; the scene plays itself out all the time. When you have spent as much time in the asylum as I have, everything becomes clockwork to you. "Not true," mouths Thomas, "just haven't found her, is all. Just haven't found my dog."

I should look away, but cannot. Call it morbid fascination. I have been accused of worse. "She's dead, Mr. Thomas. You killed her. Her and all the dogs in your neighborhood."

"Not true."

"Afraid so. You poisoned them. All the dogs that ever pissed on your lawn. Poisoned and gone."

"Nah, not true! That was never me. I never did such a thing."

Benny rubs Thomas' shoulder, feigning comfort. Benny is everyone's friend; he manipulates the emotionally broken, conforms their reality to suit his own. Such is his way; I have always despised it. "Umm, yeah, you did," Benny smirks, lips heavy with sin. Squeezes harder upon Thomas' shoulder and the forlorn man grimaces. "You killed them all. Lots of them. Motherfucker. You killed defenseless dogs, Mr. Thomas. I read that they never stood a chance. Including your own."

"That was never me. Never. Never. *Never*!"

The scene plays itself out again; nothing more than rote. "Motherfucker," Benny spits, "how could you kill your own dog?"

Anguish ruptures Thomas' face. I cannot look away. "Not possible. I love her!"

"Yep, you must've loved her death whimper, too. Tell me, did you hold her, at least? Did you hold your dog after you poisoned her? Tell me about her death rattle, Mr.

Thomas... tell me how she pissed in your arms as she croaked."

Into trembling hands, Thomas buries his face. Neither an admission of innocence nor guilt; all these years, and Thomas' sentence still hangs in this decayed air. "No," Thomas says weakly. "She can't piss if she's cold."

The first blow arrives in the form of an open palm. It is ferocious; Thomas' neck snaps to the side, ear red as a beet. The second blow catches him in the temple; a balled fist, now Thomas' eyes roll endlessly, searching, searching for his long lost dog. Benny grabs him under his armpits, stands him up. Thomas can barely keep his balance. Benny seizes him by the throat; Thomas' arms flay like a silly, frail mannequin.

Silly, frail mannequin, when will you learn that you cannot fight?

Benny punches Thomas flush in the face; knees and nose buckle under its force. Another shot—quick, relentless, vicious. It is a small wonder that anything remains of Thomas' nose at all. I have lost count how many times it has been busted. I have lost count how many times his will has been strung out to die.

The assault still does not cease. Thomas, helpless in Benny's viselike grip, legs staggering under each blow; left eye, a gruesome shade of purple, swollen shut. Brow split; two teeth knocked clear from his gums. Another jagged through his upper lip. Benny pauses, wipes his fist along his stark, white jacket, gaze lingering upon the fresh, ruddy streaks. "You've gotten my coat dirty," he says matter-of-factly. Benny always wears a clean jacket, much cleaner than the other orderlies. He is not going to be pleased about this.

But as his elbow rears back, fist aimed for a final, crushing blow, he hears anguished cries echoing from down the hall, followed by Arnold's excited yells.

***

If only these walls could speak.

But they do not horde the secrets one would assume. Within this asylum, secrets are nonexistent. It is the perception of reality that is cloaked; the basic functions of humanity long swept under the rug.

The asylum accepted me many years ago. My journey began on a gurney, like so many of the others. Stripped of necessities, drained of all money and clothes, of my wants, of needs, of threadbare hope. My soul, however... my soul the bastards left intact. Yes, like so many of the others. Within this debased place known as the asylum, that is the cruelest punishment of all.

I have inhabited this place for so long that I pass freely to and fro, passing through splintered doorways, through decaying and mold ravished rooms, always keeping mute company with its dazed residents. They do not wish to speak with me; nor do they wish to hurry me away. I am there, my presence silently acknowledged, and that seems to be enough.

Melissa sees me but wishes she did not. Her guilty conscious always toying with her, corroding her mind. She is a sweet girl. Simply misunderstood. Are we not all? Savagely she swipes her right arm over left, razor blade shaking between pinched fingers. Melissa thinks she stole it from the orderly. She thinks he absentmindedly left it upon her desk during rounds.

I observe her, say nothing. I will not judge. It is not my place. I think she is thankful for that in some small way. Unhindered she continues to cut, my everlasting silence serving as both comfort and fuel.

"What's going on today, Missy?" The orderly's voice is jovial, seemingly warm. But I hear it the way blood would seep. A coldhearted douche. He stands in the splintered doorway, one of the splintered doorways I have passed through for all these years, and smiles. He smiles, and I ignore him. He ignores me. The orderlies, they have tired of my antics some time ago.

"Nothing much," Melissa grins as the rusted blade slices through scar tissue, as the blood that sounds like the orderly's voice bubbles to the surface of her pale skin. She likes pain. Without shame, I admit I like it as well.

Samuel—I know he likes pain more than we both do. More than he should. He watches intently as her blade sinks deeper. He will not fess up to it, but he very much admires Melissa. The way she carves her story across her canvas of flesh—it is an art, self-expression he has denied himself. He will not confess that he is scared to do so; a man such as Samuel will never confess a want for anything.

Melissa searches for a fresh swath along her forearm, finds a dulled intersection of scars. She rips the razor across her skin—harried strokes— as Samuel steps from the doorway, tongue flicking over his lips. I can see the gleam in his eye. "Doesn't look like it's nothing much," breath short. Roused.

She glances at him; I suppose when you are a good cutter, you do not need to watch what you are doing. Then turns away. "Just doing stuff," she replies absently.

Samuel nods. Tongue wagging. "Can I... can I help you with your... stuff?"

She stops cutting. The blood drips from her arm in slow little beads. Paints the darker stains upon the floor.

Those stains have been there a long time. Longer than I have been here. Melissa stares at those stains. Blood pitter-patters, pitter-patters. "Sure."

At first, he approaches awkwardly, cautiously. Samuel is nothing more than a wolf in sheep's clothing. He reaches suddenly, hand steady as a rock. "May I?" he asks politely. *Oh Samuel, what big teeth you have.*

Samuel takes the razor from her hands, smiles as her blood smears his fingertips. Regards it, admiring the pitting along its edge, a tiny chink missing from the blade. Swings his gaze from girl to blade to girl again, tongue protruding from the corner of his mouth. Then he swipes. Blade kisses Melissa's cheek. She jumps from the chair, palm seeking her newest wound.

Samuel lunges, seizes her hair and with a violent snap drives her to her knees. Another snap; her chin juts to the ceiling, throat exposed, eyes pleading. Pleading. They both plead for the pain. He presses the razor behind her ear, nibbling his lower lip as she does the same. He is hard; erection inches from her face, but sexual gratification is furthest from his mind. Swiftly the blade descends as Melissa cries out.

I do not act as he slashes her neck and face. I do not act as the blood endlessly drips upon the dark stained floor.

He releases her and staggers backward, boots slipping in the shallows of Melissa's blood. His hand, wrist, now splattered in crimson; that dark smile of his continuing to spread. "That," he starts, and wipes her blood over his lips, lapping them dry with probing tongue, "was incredible." He stares at the blade again, stares at Melissa upon her knees, cheek and brow now red ribbons hanging from her face. "Simply fucking incredible."

Melissa says nothing. Eventually she tilts her chin, offering her throat once more.

Samuel staggers, flush with excitement. "Yes," he whispers, squeezing himself through his pants and brings the blade down to her throat. "Good God, girl, yes. *Yes!*"

When will they learn that God never belonged here?

Eyelids fluttering, she folds her hands upon her lap. Her face will heal in time. It has before. But she has never experienced the flow of her essence in such a delicious stream of finality. She thinks today could be that day.

I do not act as the blade punctures her flesh. I do not act as Samuel freezes, startled by the frantic screams of Arnold echoing down the hall.

***

If only these walls could speak.

But they do. For many years, the walls of this asylum have spoken, whispering tales of madness and betrayal. Singing sweet tunes of solitude and death. No one comes to this asylum to live. Not the ones who work here. Not the ones sentenced here. For day by day, hour by hour, this asylum absorbs their darkness as its own, savoring every morsel, sucking their corrupted humanity as marrow from bone, accepting the gifts of suffering and despair that bloat the air with a glorious indifference.

Samuel hustles down the hall, nearly falling over Benny's crumpled form in the splintered doorway to Gloria's room.

Yes, all these doorways are splintered. So much like these broken, despondent souls.

Gloria has not stopped talking since her first day in this asylum. Muttering, incessantly muttering, but how I have grown fond of her.

"I... hear..."

"What the hell is going on, man?" Benny, eyes wild, imploring. "What the hell is going on?" Curiously, Benny's soiled jacket is the first thing to grab Samuel's attention. He knows that Benny always wears a clean jacket. Always much cleaner than the other orderlies.

Samuel does not answer. Absently, he swats Benny's shaking hand away and steps into the room.

He sees Arnold struggling to pry a white heap from the opposite wall. Samuel shakes his head in confusion. "Stop fucking around, Arnold," he orders, then quickly realizes it is not a white heap at all. The razor blade slips from his fingers.

Gloria hangs several feet above the floor, cheek grotesquely attached to the wall. *"I hear,"* she coos joyously.

Arnold strains, a bony ankle in each of his hands. He tugs in vain. "Help me!" he shouts, but Samuel does not answer. "Dammit, help me get this bitch down, man!"

"I hear... I hear them all... inside all this while... time for me to move on... time for me to go," Gloria laughs, suddenly so mocking, so defiant. For the first time since this asylum claimed her, so happy.

Arnold pulls with all his strength, but she does not budge. "Help me, Samuel!"

It starts with an odd slurping, like animals feeding from a trough. Samuel hears it first and turns to Benny, who remains fetal upon the floor, eyes squeezed shut. Behind him, patients now slowly mill, filling the hall. Samuel looks back to Arnold, who drops Gloria's ankles from his grasp.

Clots of Gloria's hair drop along the wall as the sucking intensifies; she half-screams, half-cries in delirium, one cloudy eye still free of the wall spinning inside its socket, until the skin of her brow flops over it like some obscene parchment. Wet, hungry gurgling fills the room, and rivulets of blood spider web along the wall. An awful pop and Gloria's flesh rends free from her skull; a mask of skin hanging from her neck, a grotesque hood of glistening pulp. Within seconds her head half-sinks into the wall, lipless jaws still chattering.

Arnold retches across his feet. The denizens of this asylum push stoically into Gloria's room, stepping over the incoherent form of Benny, forming a loose circle behind Samuel. With dulled expressions, they gaze at the wall—Thomas, Melissa, the lot of them—staggering shoulder to shoulder, listening impassively to the awful separation of muscle from bone.

I do not act. There is no need for me to do so. This asylum has flourished through the years governed under its own rules, self-sustained by its own set of laws. I do not act as fists and feet pummel Benny, punching, kicking and tearing at his limbs; I do not act as Thomas slams Benny's head against an unyielding floor until life leaks from his ears. I do not act as hands hold captive a struggling Samuel, and Melissa carves from ear to ear a ragged line across his throat with yet another razor she has stolen. I do not act as Arnold collapses under the horde's weight, as angry, writhing bodies slowly snuff his life by jamming stinking washcloths deep into his mouth. The orderlies' bodies will be cast later into the incinerator, once the floors have been scrubbed and toweled dry. The patients of this asylum know just what to do.

What remains of Gloria drops in a wet heap; skin, mostly, the occasional shard of bone. At last, she is free to pass to and fro as I have for so many, many years. For only now does she realize her deliverance has come; only now does she realize she has become part of the hierarchy, and that the walls here feed not on evil but the tortured essence of the souls it protects.

If only these walls could speak.

But *we* do. And the forgotten residents of this asylum patiently await our calling.

COUNT NEFARIO

Tom Howard

"I prefer being called Count Nefario," said the strange little man with bright yellow hair.

Dr. Imogene Stone smiled, glancing around at the other members of the therapy group, aware everyone was watching her. "We've discussed this before, Mr. Doe. Think how disruptive it would be if we all hid behind nicknames."

"It's not a nickname," he said. "It's the title I took when I became a super-villain to strike terror into the hearts of my enemies." His voice grew louder and his pale face redder.

"Yes, a super-villain. Please control yourself, Mr. Doe. You don't want to spend the session in a straitjacket again, do you?"

He slunk down in his chair and didn't answer.

"Now where were we yesterday? Angela was telling us about her purple teddy bear and Mr. Doe was telling us about the world he was from. Again." She pointedly opened her notebook, poised her pen, and stared at the strange man expectantly.

He sighed. "It's not another world," he said. "It's this world, only different."

"Yes, so you've said. On your world, you're from the United States of the Americas and not the United States of America?"

"My country is called the United States of North America and includes what you call Mexico and Canada."

She looked at her notes, searching his descriptions from the previous sessions for discrepancies. As always, his delusion was pervasive and consistent. "And your parents were from a continent called West America?"

"Yes," he replied. "That's where I was before I was dumped here."

"I was abducted by aliens the last time I was in West America," said Mrs. Lentz, not looking up from her pretend knitting. Although they'd taken away her potentially harmful needles, she still felt the need to create imaginary and unfinished scarves, hats, and sweaters. "They probed me real good."

"Thank you, Clara," said Dr. Stone in her commanding warden voice. "Let's let Mr. Doe speak now."

The little man glanced at the old woman. "Why don't you help her?" he asked. "Isn't that your job?"

"I thought I was a cave shaman, Mr. Doe, drilling holes in patients' heads to release evil spirits?" She glanced down at her earlier notes. "Or was I a nefarious member of an organization called the Crime Lords?"

When he didn't answer, she tried a new approach. "What would a doctor do for her on your world, I mean, your dimension?"

"Not just her," he said, "all these people – except Angela."

She looked at a blushing young woman sitting in the circle of plastic chairs. A man was leaning against her. "Mr. O'Hara, do you think it's a good idea to be sitting beside Miss Atkinson? You know how…excitable you get."

The middle-aged man grinned sheepishly and moved to an empty seat beside an old man who was busy staring at the ceiling and twitching. Dr. Stone wondered how much longer Mr. Snell's meds would help his spasms and checked his folder. Yes, it was at the upper limit – anymore and he'd be completely immobilized. She made a note that he might be the next candidate for the catatonia clinic upstate. She'd have to check and see if he was a paying customer or state supported. The more freeloaders she got off the books, the earlier she could retire and the wealthier she would be.

She was making a note when Mr. Doe stood up. He walked over to Mr. Luckinbill who was shuffling his deck of cards. Some people smiled when they were in their happy place, Mr. Luckinbill shuffled. He didn't complain as Mr. Doe took the cards and continued shuffling them. With a turn and a flip of his wrists, Mr. Doe sent them cascading at Mr. Snell. The old man howled and jumped to his feet as the cards harmlessly hit him. Before the orderly could react, the man grabbed his chair and threw it at Mr. Doe.

Who caught it easily and sat it back in the circle. The orderly, keeping his eye on Mr. Doe, helped the old man back to his chair.

"Mr. Doe!" The doctor's stern voice made several patients flinch. "Do you need to be restrained?"

"No, Doctor. I was proving a point."

"I don't understand."

"Of course you don't." He crossed his arms and looked at Mr. Snell. The old man was glaring at everyone. "If you did, you'd have noticed that he's stopped shaking."

She hadn't noticed but it was obvious after he pointed it out. The old man was breathing heavily but not twitching.

"You wish you were smart enough to be a Crime Lord," muttered Mr. Doe, taking his own seat. "This poor guy will never get any better with you taking care of him."

She ignored Mr. Doe's insults, intrigued by Mr. Snell's steady hands. "Why did throwing a deck of cards at him improve his condition?"

"Think about it, Doctor. It wasn't the cards. It was the chair. If I have to take you back to grade school psychiatry, I'll never get out of here and back home."

"His fight or flight response." she realized. "He thought you were attacking him, so he reacted. He fought back."

"We'll get you up to community college level yet, Dr. Stone. That's exactly right. Where I come from, they'd diagnose him using personality panes. Lives are split into windows or panes and stacked like dominos – the Baby Pane, Toddler Pane, etc. You've been trying to fix a broken pane by putting tape on the one that is six or sixteen panes away."

"You don't know why he's stuck between fighting or running away?"

He shrugged. "No. That's your job."

He stood up and indicated his fellow patients. "I'm probably breaking about a million inter-dimensional laws telling you this, but on Superworld none of these people would be here, except maybe Angela because her brain seems to have stopped growing at an early age."

She made a note. It was the first time he'd given his delusionary home world a name. "How do you know so much about psychiatry on your world, Mr. Doe? Are you a doctor?"

He smiled. "No. I have, however, spent time in several of our finer mental institutions."

"I see. Sounds like your world isn't perfect after all."

"Of course it isn't," he said, taking his seat. "I started out as an orphaned petty thief, using my superior intellect to outwit the police. After getting caught, the authorities thought I might yet become a benefit to society. I was doing that during a battle in West America when someone zapped me and forced me here."

He looked around the room at the other patients staring at him. The old man had started to twitch again. "Go ahead, Doctor. Buy into my delusions for just a minute and ask me the important questions about panes. I could be yanked back home as quickly as I was brought here, and you'll never know how to help these folks."

She didn't want to enable his delusions, but she was curious and did have questions.

"Explain this window process to me. Please." She turned to a clean page in her notebook and waited, telling herself that she was obtaining more information concerning the extent of his delusionary state.

"It's not my process," he said. He moved to Brian. The man was staring at Angela with his mouth open. "I'd guess this guy's mom did something to him when he was a child. You'll never fix him by working on him as an adult."

"I see," said Dr. Stone. "On your world, doctors can travel back in time to where the trauma took place and stop it. Very advanced. However, until such a time as people on this world can—"

"You're sliding all the way back to kindergarten psychiatry, Doctor," he said with a frown. "Think. How do you normally make a person relive a traumatic event in their past?"

"Hypnosis. Role-playing," she answered automatically. She realized that she was losing control of the session, a dangerous thing with an intelligent patient like Mr. Doe, a man completely out of touch with reality.

"Very entertaining, Mr. Doe. Please take your seat."

"Don't you want to know more?"

Dr. Stone nodded at the orderly. "Please take your seat, Mr. Doe. I won't ask again." She had to regain control.

Mr. Doe bristled. "These people don't have a prayer if they're relying on a drugged up quack like you. How many tranquilizers have you had today? How much time does Grandpa Twitchy have before you fry his brain with electroshock or drugs and send him off to the catatonia ward upstate?"

She jumped to her feet, her folders flying everywhere. "That's quite enough of that, Mr. Doe! I don't know who told you those lies. Orderly, escort everyone to their rooms please. We're done for today."

The self-professed super-villain turned quickly and joined the others as they filed out, but Dr. Stone saw the quick smile that crossed his face. She counted her breaths until the room was cleared and picked up her papers, feeling irritated with herself that she'd lost control so easily.

The next afternoon Dr. Stone was late for the afternoon group therapy session because she'd worked with individual patients in the morning and then tried to make her ward rounds before the therapy session.

She ignored Mr. Doe as she glanced at the small circle of six men and opened her folders. She didn't want him to think he deserved special treatment.

"I'm sorry that I'm late, gentlemen. I've had a busy morning, so let's get to work. I believe Mr. Porter was telling us of his need for continual validation when dealing with his alcoholism and drug addictions." She looked expectantly at the large man sitting opposite her, pointedly ignoring Mr. Doe and his half smile.

"Well," said Mr. Porter, "As long as I have people around me, I don't drink as much. I don't do any drugs when I'm happy. It's when I'm all by myself for any length of time that I need a little something to get me through the day."

"Excellent, Mr. Porter. Now have you considered some of the coping mechanisms I suggested to help you with those times when you are alone and feel isolated?"

"Yes," he said, "and Mr. Doe has been helping me."

She didn't want to ask. The troubles of her morning had been caused by her foolishly listening to Mr. Doe and his wild theories. "What did he recommend?"

"He suggested I think back to a time when I didn't need stimulants, a time when I was alone but okay with it. The only time I could think of was the summer I spent with my grandmother. We were stuck out in the boonies, and I had to read all of her Louis l'Amour books for entertainment."

"That's very interesting," said Dr. Stone, "but I think we should deal with more professional recommendations, don't you?" She smiled, waiting until the entire group was focused on her.

"Yes." he said, "but I went to the clinic library and checked out a few books. When I went to my room and read some terrible old Westerns, guess what happened? No cravings!"

The other men in the circle smiled and nodded.

"Well, Mr. Doe," she said, at last turning to him, "perhaps you should be sitting in this chair." She felt herself growing angry and realized she'd forgotten to take her medicine in her rush to get to the session. She'd had a rough night and morning, and the day was proving as difficult. "Perhaps you could use one of your other-world procedures on all the patients. Although we wouldn't want anyone to end up like Mr. Snell, would we?"

Mr. Doe didn't inquire about Mr. Snell. He stared at her for a moment and said, "Is that a new hairdo, Doctor? Or perhaps you didn't go home last night and slept on a cot in your office. Working on some new theory for psychiatric methods, perhaps?" His wide smile made her grit her teeth.

She didn't reply. He knew she had tried his pane theory. Did he know she'd spent all night sketching out what the procedure would entail? She was a visual person and had a stack of diagrams showing what she believed the pane process would look like from birth to death. She'd been sucked into Mr. Doe's fantasy. Like a fool, she'd summoned Mr. Snell to her office to try an experiment. If the pane process had worked on him, she would've had something for publication – something completely new and provable. She and her clinic would have been famous.

Instead she had created a twitching vegetable who'd bashed his head against the wall repeatedly. She'd been a fool for listening to Mr. Doe's imaginary treatment.

The man sighed. "You didn't try to erase the trauma, did you?" He shook his head. "You should have asked me for more details if you were going to join me in my delusion, Doctor. Or would that have made it seem like I wasn't insane, that maybe I did come from somewhere else?"

She stopped taking notes.

"I would have told you that you can't erase, you can only cope with whatever happened or turn it into something else. So, is Grandpa Twitchy catatonic?"

She looked down. "That's none of your concern. Mr. Porter, the last man that Mr. Doe gave recommendations to is on suicide watch. I recommend you stick to your medications and do not rely on an untrained individual to help you with your addictive behavior. Do you agree?"

He looked at Mr. Doe before he nodded at her. She worked on other patients' issues and ignored Mr. Doe the rest of the session. She didn't let his small smile bother her. Much. *Had he given her just enough information to make a fool of her? Was he manipulating her somehow, purposely pulling her into his delusion?* She couldn't tell what his motives were. *Why tell her about the pane process if he knew she was going to endanger someone?*

Perhaps he hadn't cared that she might hurt Mr. Snell – he just wanted to see if she'd dance to his tune. With a twinge of guilt, she realized that she hadn't cared about Mr. Snell's well-being either. All she wanted was her name in a publication and a reason to raise her rates.

At the end of the day, she checked on Mr. Snell in the suicide ward. His head was bandaged, he was heavily tranquilized, and he wasn't responsive. *How was she going to explain this to the state inspectors when they came through?* She took a few tranquilizers, grabbed a snack from the vending machines, and fell into her cot for some troubled sleep.

She dreamt she was sitting on a throne. She was wearing a gold and maroon suit with bells sewn onto the hems. Cartoony bank robbers were bowing to her as they dropped bags of money onto the floor at her feet. Of course, they had big dollar signs printed on them.

"What is this place?" she asked a servant with bright yellow hair.

"This is where you always wanted to be," said Mr. Doe. "Rich and powerful. Ah, here comes your tailor."

A woman with the same hair color as Mr. Doe made her way through the thugs, dragging a peach-colored sack behind her. "I've almost got it finished, dear," said the woman, flipping the sack around so Dr. Stone could see it fully. It was an empty body. It looked like a deflated blow-up doll.

The woman cackled as she spread it out. "You won't have to count on that lab coat to cover your broadening hips, Your Highness. Your new body will be thin and curvy in all the right places. Are you sure about this brown hair color? I could sew in something red or blonde just as easily."

Dr. Stone was speechless.

"What's the matter?" asked Mr. Doe, picking up a saggy hand and rubbing it gently. "Power, money, beauty, and sex appeal. Isn't that what you wanted?"

Mr. Snell stumbled into the room, his head split open and blood gushing in improbable amounts down his body. He was still twitching.

"Get him out of here," barked Mr. Doe, and several of the bank robbers swiftly carried him out the door. "We don't care about him. Do we, Doctor?"

A bell chimed loudly and all the men lined up, one behind the other, from the doorway to the throne. When the bell chimed again, the man nearest the door fell forward, knocking down the man in front of him. That man started a chain reaction and all the men fell like dominos, falling toward Dr. Stone with alarming speed. She tried to jump up but she was stuck to the gaudy throne. The last man fell toward her, and she reached up without thinking and placed her index finger in the middle of his forehead. He froze, inches from her. She pushed him back.

Incredibly, the man who'd fallen sprang back upright, causing the man behind him to stand. It continued around the room until all the men were once again standing in a line.

Mr. Doe looked stunned. "How interesting. That's not supposed to happen." He put his hand on his chin and studied the line of standing men before he turned to the doctor. "Tell me, Dr. Stone. You weren't adopted were you? Ever feel like you came from...somewhere else?"

"Dr. Stone," he said but it didn't sound like his voice. She awoke to find the nurse standing over her.

"Dr. Stone," said the nurse as the doctor sat up. "I'm glad you're in the clinic already. Someone's been in the janitor closet again. Mr. Carlson says it's a mess when he comes in to do his work in the morning."

Dr. Stone swung her feet to the floor and looked at the clock. It was barely 6 a.m. "Change the locks. Keep the key in the safe."

"I'll need Dr. Wheeler's authorization for the purchase order."

"Fine. He should be at Kelly's Bar around noon. You might be able to catch him before he falls off his stool." Dr. Wheeler was her partner in the run-down mental institution. "Can you get me a cup of coffee?"

"Certainly, Doctor," said the woman as if noticing for the first time that Dr. Stone was sleeping in her office. "It'll be at the nurses' station."

"I'll pick it up after I check on Mr. Snell."

The nurse's face tightened. "I'm sorry, Doctor, but he…didn't make it."

"What?" she asked, forcing herself to her feet. "When?"

"Around midnight. I'm sorry."

Dr. Stone shook her head, excused the nurse, and headed to her private bathroom, grateful it had a shower and a stocked medicine cabinet. She'd need more than coffee this morning.

Afterward, she signed the required paperwork and watched them move Mr. Snell's body to the ambulance that would take the old man's remains to the funeral parlor. She took a deep breath and made a decision – Mr. Doe was going to be the next patient moved to the catatonia clinic upstate.

She was still looking forward to it when Mr. Doe was escorted in for his ten o'clock private appointment with her.

The man sat in the chair on the other side of her desk but didn't speak. His usual smirk was gone, and he looked at her with an expression of defeat as the orderly left to stand outside the door.

"Good morning, Mr. Doe," she said, putting on her professional face. "Did you sleep well?"

He sighed. "Okay, do we have to play this game? You don't believe me. I don't trust you. Just send me back to my room and I'll be quiet."

"Oh, I see," she said with a smile. "You're going to be the nice Mr. Doe today."

"I'm sorry about Mr. Snell. I should have realized you'd try something. I forgot you've been the queen of this domain for years."

She sighed. "I'm sorry about Mr. Snell, too. I was just looking at his file this morning. His family was killed in an automobile accident when he was driving. He was thrown clear but couldn't save them."

"Instead of having him think he'd saved them and they'd moved away or something," said Mr. Doe, "you just ripped the memory out of his mind and left him confused as to what had happened to his family. You gave him nothing to live for."

She smiled. "So if we're going to be adult colleagues today, what am I going to do with you?"

"I suspect I'm on the next ambulance to Comatose City," he said with a grin. "Unless I can convince you to let me go."

"I don't understand," she said, leaning back. "A smart man like you, you could just walk out of here."

"And the police would pick me up by sunset. I want a clean bill of mental health so I can start finding my way home."

She started to correct him but restrained herself. For once, she'd play along. "So, you want your freedom to find your way home."

He nodded. "And in return, I'd help you with the pane process. When I discovered it had been used on me, I did extensive research on it. I'll give you everything I have. Isn't that what you want?"

"What I want?" She thought about it. "I used to think I wanted to change the world, Mr. Doe, and fix everyone. Now, I just want to survive in one piece until I can retire to the place in Florida that my adoptive parents left me."

"So you're a stranger in a strange land, too. It's not too late to change the world, Doctor. I can help you. You'll be famous and rich."

She smiled. "Ah, I see that you're using the carrot on me, Mr. Doe. What is your alternative should I say no? What do you intend to use for a stick?"

"I see you are smarter than I gave you credit. It's true; I manipulated you into trying the pane process on someone. I thought you would fail and have to ask me for help. Instead, you decided I'm even more insane than you originally diagnosed. You think I'm dangerous."

He glanced at the door. "You're right. I am dangerous. In ten minutes, the fire alarm will go off, caused by a fire in the janitor closet. When the patients are evacuated, I will be missing. The state inspectors will be here within twenty-four hours. They will have received an anonymous phone call saying you paid a man to burn down the clinic for the insurance."

She frowned, not liking where this conversation was going. "They'll never believe you."

"Ah, but they will. When they discover your high number of catatonic patients, your self-prescribed drug use, and Mr. Snell's recent demise, you'll be under investigation for years. That, Dr. Stone, is my big stick."

"You're mad," she said.

He laughed. "Possibly. But mad or not, I'm leaving here today. I'd like to make it as painless as possible."

She was angry but afraid. Still, she tried to placate him. "Please, let's discuss this, Mr. Doe." If worse came to worse, she could press the alarm on her desk that summoned the orderly. Mr. Doe would be medicated, placed into a straight jacket, and no longer be a problem.

"Don't over-think it, Doctor," he said, "and call me Count Nefario. You know I won't harm anyone...unless they try to stop me from getting home."

Her eyes widened and she pressed the alarm button near her left hand. Nothing happened. The orderly didn't appear.

Count Nefario nodded. "I see you've made your choice, Imogene. I'm afraid all the alarms have been disconnected except for the fire alarm." He glanced at the clock. "Which should be going off about now."

"Wait!" she exclaimed. "You'll give me all the details about your treatment...Count Nefario?"

She tried to convince herself that she was just agreeing so he'd stop his plan, but she knew what he was offering her was monumental. If there was a chance that it could actually work...

"You are a master manipulator," she said, standing and holding out her hand. "I know when I'm beaten. I'll sign the release immediately. Will it take longer than this afternoon to educate me on the details of the pane theory?"

"No," he replied, standing and shaking her hand. "I think even you can get the basics. It will take you years of clinical research to perfect, but I think you will succeed."

"Thank you. Now may I send the staff to remove the incendiary device you've set up in the janitor closet?"

He smiled. "I am a master manipulator. There will be no fire…this morning. I'll have that signed release now before you try and put me in a straightjacket. I'll let you know about the other incendiary devices after our session this afternoon. Bring your notebook."

She sat and pulled the release paperwork from her file cabinet. *Damn him. This pane process better work.*

The next day, exhausted but confident that she had the pane process down and had seen the last of Count Nefario, she started her morning therapy session.

Mr. Luckinbill was shuffling but Mrs. Lentz wasn't knitting. She sat with her hands calmly in her lap.

"Mrs. Lentz, is everything all right?" asked Dr. Stone.

"I prefer being called Madame Mystic," she said with a small smile.

VISITING HOURS

Megan Dorei

Drumbeat like gunfire raps through my mind. I dig my nails into my scalp as the percussive explosions rack my brain. The frantic beating will not stop. It's been playing in my mind for hours.

Tears flow, fast and hot, down my cheeks. I whimper, wanting to cry out but knowing I can't. If I make any noise, Kurt will come for me again, and this time he won't hesitate to use his fists.

He came at dinner time with my food and a syringe filled with bright yellow liquid. It reminded me of police tape at a crime scene. I haven't been eating for the past three days; refusing to after I realized that they were mixing some kind of medicine in with it to get us to sleep. He threatened me with the mysterious liquid, telling me that if I didn't start eating he'd fill me full of it.

I punched the tray of gray-looking food out of his hand, leaving a few bright red welts on my knuckles. I tried to scramble away before he could grab me, but his fingers gnarled in my hair and yanked me back. My neck cracked, and for one terrifying moment I thought he'd broken it. A scream ripped from my chest but it was cut off quickly as he tossed me into the wall.

The breath left my lungs in one quick rush. My stomach flattened against my spine and I dry-heaved convulsively. Through the tears, I barely had time to register the boot flying toward my face before it struck my left temple.

Blinding pain flared across my eyes. I skidded across the linoleum floor, skin ripping as it tried unsuccessfully to stick to the scuffed tile. For a moment, I couldn't see anything. I blinked my eyes several times to clear them of tears and sudden blindness.

Kurt pulled me up just as my hazy eyes cleared, popping my shoulder out of place. I cried out in pain and he grabbed my throat, choking me. He said something but I couldn't hear it through the ringing in my ears. Then he stuck the needle into my arm and pushed the plunger.

Now I'm sitting against the wall under the only window in the room besides the tiny square of glass on the door. I rock desperately back and forth as the drumming pummels me.

After- what? Hours? Days?- of this violent noise, I lift my head and open my eyes. As soon as I do, my gaping mouth closes over my tongue, and I feel a bright burst of blood against my teeth.

Stretching from my wall to the opposite wall, on either side of my curled body, is a line of young boys in black-and-steel marching uniforms. All of them are carrying marching snares and the same mindless, unblinking expressions.

They force the beat, this tribe of drumline boys. It's not just in my head.

Unfolding arthritically from my curled position, I stumble in front of the nearest drummer, waving my hands in front of his face.

"Please," I croak, hissing as a jolt of pain bursts through my dislocated shoulder. "Stop making that racket."

The drummer doesn't seem to notice me, doesn't seem to blink or move anything except his arms.

"Please, stop," I plead, wanting to reach out and snatch the drumsticks from his fists. My left arm pulses with heat. The drummer pulses with rhythm and still acts like I don't exist.

As I peer closer, opening my mouth to speak again, I realize that I can't see myself in the flat black reflection of his pupils. I gasp in horror, stumbling backwards, and land painfully on my ass. The drummer takes no notice.

A terrible thought drowns me, fills me to the brim, and suddenly I can't breathe. *What if I'm not real? What if I don't exist? Or what if I'm just a figment of someone else's shattered imagination?* My eyes grow wide with terror and my limbs pool into useless puddles on the floor.

"Help me," I croak, but I barely make a sound. There's a fuzzing sound growing in my head, like static on a TV screen. I clutch at my ears as it grows, blending with the drumbeats in a cacophony of noise.

In a sudden rush of adrenaline I scramble to my feet and race to the door. My footsteps take an eternity; the soles of my thin, ragged shoes peel from the floor as though the tiles have changed to the consistency of glue. On either side of me, the drummers hold their ground, drumsticks flying, eyes without reflection.

I slam into the door before I realize I've reached it. My body strikes the thick metal like a mallet hitting a gong. My breath fogs up the glass, lacing it with a veil of milky whiteness.

"Help!" I scream hoarsely. It breaks into the harsh noise around me but cannot overcome it.

In the hallway, Kurt is making his rounds, casually swinging the master key that he keeps on a chain at his side. At the sound of my scream, he whips around and his brown eyes meet mine. The reaction that twists his lips is halfway between a grin and a snarl.

With that terrible grimace plastered on his pale face, he saunters to my door, still swinging that damn chain, until he is right up against the glass.

I scream at him and pound against the glass, but he just stares at me. I slap my palms against the metal until they turn bright red. I punch my knuckles into its unyielding surface until they bleed. But still he stares and does nothing.

I'm not sure exactly when I black out. I don't remember crumpling to the floor, only blinking open my eyes at the gentle touch of someone's hand on my chin.

He stares at me with the greenest eyes I've ever seen. I blink at him several times, mouth gaping slightly, because they are like the fields I used to play in as a child when I would visit my grandpa. He lived alone in an old farmhouse a few counties from my hometown, and every summer he would grow wheat on his fifty acres. When it was young and green, I would dive into it like it was an ocean and disappear.

That's how I feel now, staring into this stranger's eyes. Like I'm swimming in an ocean, disappearing. *Do I really exist? Does it matter?*

"Ellyn," the stranger says. His voice is low and gruff, like striking a match, yet it's strangely comforting.

"How do you know my name?" I whisper. My voice floats from far away.

"Ellyn, give me your arm," the man demands, holding out his hand. It is worn and dirty and dotted with freckles.

I hold out my left arm in a daze, still staring at his eyes. He takes it, wrapping my wrist in rough warmth, and presses his other hand to my shoulder. His eyes refocus on mine.

"Hold still," he commands quietly. Then he tugs.

Blinding pain clears me of my haze, like jumping into ice water. A small cry escapes my lips, but before it can transform into a full scream the man presses his hand over my mouth. I blink at him through the tears, shocked and betrayed. He shakes his head at me.

"Have to be quiet," he says sternly. With a small warning glance, he tugs on my arm again.

This time, with the pain, there is a shockingly loud pop as my shoulder rolls back into place. As the pain fades, my body slowly relaxes, relieved to have the maddening soreness removed.

Green-eyes takes his hand from my mouth and releases me. Standing, he looks down at me and raises an eyebrow. The florescent lights make his rich auburn curls burn red.

He blinks slowly at me and then extends his hand. Delicately I place mine in his and allow him to pull me to my feet.

"Who are you?" I breathe. My voice is shallow and cannot rise above a whisper.

"Soren," he murmurs. His eyes never leave mine.

"Soren," I repeat under my breath. "What are you doing here?"

He shrugs. "Visiting you."

I stare at him for a long time, neither of us speaking. I have never seen this man before in my life. I don't know how he knows me, or how he got here, or why he would visit me. In that moment, I don't care.

Besides the guards who come to check up on me, I haven't seen another human being in three years. It's a breath of fresh air to see a new face. There's something about him- something I can't place- that comforts me.

After a moment, I realize that the room is quiet, eerily so. My head whips back and forth, searching for the drummers, and Soren follows me with his eyes.

"Where are they?" I ask thoughtlessly.

"The drummers?" Soren replies.

I look at him sharply. "Yes…how did you know?"

He ignores my question. "You need to rest," he says, taking my hand and guiding me to the stark white bed in the corner. "You have a long journey ahead of you."

I furrow my brows in confusion. "What do you mean?" I ask, crawling obediently into bed.

"You'll see," he says simply. Soren presses gently on my chest, pushing me down into the mattress. A sudden flood of exhaustion washes through me at his touch and my eyelids flutter tiredly.

The room grows hazy, thick, but just as I'm drifting off to sleep I remember something.

"Thank you," I mumble through heavy, slurring lips. "For my shoulder."

I think I hear Soren chuckle but that might have been my imagination.

***

When I open my eyes, the panic leaks in slowly. Things move slowly, as though everything has been filled with lead. The sleepy haze leaves my eyes like molasses, and when I try to lift my hand to rub it away I find that I can't move any of my limbs.

"Doctor," a woman's voice says from somewhere near my left temple. I try to crane my neck to see her, but it's like trying to lift a mountain. "She's awake."

"Thank you, Claire," a man replies, stepping into view.

He is dressed in the all-white asylum garb, red-and-gold flower insignia steam-pressed above his heart. Though the white jacket flares out, I can tell from his lanky fingers and thin neck that he is a skinny man. His thin-rimmed, perfectly circular glasses make him look like a turtle.

"Good morning, Ellyn," he says, leaning over me.

Hello, turtle-face, I think, wishing spitefully that I could work my mouth.

"We're just going to run a few tests, alright? You see, what we've done here is given you a special form of morphine that we've been working on," he continues.

Suspicion ripples through me. *Are you **allowed** to work on new drugs, turtle-face?* I want to ask.

"Now, can you blink your eyes for me, Ellyn?" the doctor asks. I resent his tone, like he's talking to a two-year-old, but I blink all the same.

He nods. "Good. Now, just stay calm. And if you start to feel pain, blink twice for me, alright?"

Panic flares in my chest and tightens my throat. The urge to jump up from the bed and run is so strong it almost feels like pain. *Maybe I should blink twice,* I think without much humor.

I watch, panic growing, as a young blonde woman- *Claire,* I think- steps into view and hands Doctor Turtle-face a scalpel. The silver blade gleams in the cold wash of light, winking devilishly.

I squirm and writhe and struggle against the invisible holds on my body, but the movement all seems to be contained in my head. As I watch, Turtle-face presses the scalpel a few inches above the crease in my arm and slices it cleanly through the skin.

I don't feel any pain. Just the brief cold touch of the blade followed by an uncomfortable flow of warmth as my blood spills. Turtle-face looks at me expectantly and I glare at him without blinking.

Next he moves to my palm, slicing neatly across in one stroke. Still there is no pain, but the warmth of the blood pooling in my hand makes me feel nauseous.

He makes cuts in the same places on my right arm, and then moves to my legs. He makes a small incision just above both knees and slices horizontal lines across my soles. No pain.

"Alright, Ellyn, we're almost done here," Turtle-face says, lifting the scalpel from my foot. I watch as a bead of blood runs down the edge of the blade and falls to the floor. The room spins a little on its axis and I swallow hard, trying to soothe my uneasy stomach.

When he draws up my white shirt to expose my belly, the room tilts sickeningly.

What the fuck are you doing? I scream, but of course he can't hear me. Everything I do is in my head. I watch, helpless, as he presses the blade to the space just above my bellybutton.

"Ellyn!" a gruff voice barks, startling me.

My eyes flicker to the shape standing at the foot of my bed. Soren glares down at me, furiously, sternly. My eyes grow wide in amazement.

"Ellyn, don't let them do this," he growls.

I can't do anything to stop them, I think desperately. To my surprise, he seems to hear me.

"Yes, you can. Move."

I can't.

"You can."

Doctor Turtle-face draws the blade across my belly. A sting of pain brings tears to my eyes, and when he looks at me this time I blink.

He frowns. "Hmm," he hums. "That hurt?"

Hell yes, that hurt, you dumb shit!

Without pause, he moves the blade an inch from the first cut and presses down. I feel Soren tense and glance at him.

"Feel the pain, Ellyn," he instructs me.

Soren, I can't. I can't feel anything! I shout.

The scalpel cuts deep this time, recapturing my attention. I grit my teeth as desperate tears blur the doctor's face.

He lifts the scalpel slightly, pausing. "Interesting," he murmurs thoughtfully. Then he presses the knife once more to my belly, an inch above his last incision.

Soren slams his hands down on the end of the bed, rattling me. "Ellyn!" he shouts. At the same time, the blade digs into my skin, sending sharp bolts of pain up my nerve endings.

I grit my teeth and close my eyes, muscles tightening defensively. The pain travels through me, exploding, filling every cell in my body. At the end of the bed, Soren shouts one more time.

"Ellyn, scream!"

The scream rips from me, shattering my invisible shackles, so powerful my body convulses from it. The pain explodes from my lips, leaving me feeling blissfully cool. The razor edge of the blade disappears as Turtle-face jumps backwards in surprise. And still I continue to scream, kicking my legs and slamming my fists.

"Ellyn! Ellyn, calm down," Turtle-face says, attempting to sound soothing. As he leans toward me, scalpel still gripped in hand, I slap his hand away and reach for his throat.

Claire's long red fingernails dig into my wrist and catch me before I can grab the doctor's neck. She draws blood, and I scream at that pain, too.

"Sedative! I need the sedative!" she shouts. As I thrash, I catch glimpses of another girl with long, dark hair dressed in the same nurse's garb as Claire. She rushes over, brushing past Turtle-face, who is staring at me as if he can't look away.

Claire holds me down while the dark-haired nurse pulls a syringe from a red belt around her white dress and sticks the needle in my arm. I struggle against them, but the sedative works quickly through my system. My limbs grow heavy again, useless, and the room turns fuzzy and indistinct.

"Fascinating," Turtle-face breathes, staring at me with a mixture of shock and confusion. Disgust rises in me like bile but is quickly pressed down by the sedative.

"Ellyn," Soren murmurs. The urgency in his voice catches me off guard. I turn slowly to look at him, barely able to distinguish him through the veil of haziness.

"Don't fall asleep," he continues.

I…I can't…help it…

"Stay awake. I'll help you…"

But Soren's voice fades into the background of existence, along with everything else.

***

Soren doesn't let me sleep long. Just a few minutes, enough for the doctor and his nurses to leave. Then he comes around to the side of my bed and slaps me hard across the face.

The pain explodes in my head, stinging in my cheek, but I feel it from far away. The sedative is a heavy thickness within me, weighing me down. I try to glare at him but it's pretty weak.

"Why…did you do…that?" I huff.

"You need to stay awake," Soren urges me. His green eyes glitter.

I try to ask him why he's so determined to keep me awake, but my mouth feels like mush and it takes all my strength just to move my lips. I give up, sinking into the pillow.

But Soren will not let me rest. He keeps me awake by tickling my toes or pinching my arms. The exhaustion rides me, tries to pull me under, but Soren is having none of it.

Finally- hours later it must be- I feel the sedative start to wear off. My eyes still are heavy and sting like hell, but I'm awake.

Soren stares at me. I don't think he ever blinks. "You're awake," he states.

I narrow my eyes. "Yeah, no shit," I growl. "Why was it so damn important for me to stay awake, huh? Do you know how exhausted I am right now?"

"I brought you something," Soren says, ignoring my questions.

That catches me off guard. I blink at him, surprised. "You...brought me something?" I repeat, raising myself to a sitting position.

He nods, and for the first time he smiles. It looks good on him; two laugh lines form creases around his sparkling green eyes. Soren holds out a small white bag.

After a moment, I take it, curiosity winning out over my initial shock. I open it up eagerly and the sweet scent of pastries floats out. Inside is the largest Danish I've ever seen, a circle of fried bread with a pile of cream cheese in the center. My mouth waters immediately.

"Oh my God," I say, pulling the pastry from its bag. I dig in quickly, stuffing my mouth with its sweetness. At the taste, my legs go weak and a small moan bursts from my lips. I turn to Soren, eyes shining with gratitude.

"How did you know I love these?" I ask breathlessly, stealing another huge bite.

He shrugs, still smiling. "I just know things," he says.

Soren watches me as I eat, sitting down beside me on the bed. This is the most delicious thing I've tasted in years. The beauty of such a pastry washes through me, as well as the nostalgia, and I almost feel a little sad eating it.

As I'm finishing my last bite, Soren finally speaks. "Ellyn, there are some things we need to discuss," he says. His voice is solemn, the smile gone.

My chewing slows nearly to a standstill. "What do you mean?" I ask after a long pause, and swallow down the rest of my treat.

"It's time, Ellyn," he says.

My brows furrow. "Time for what?"

"Time for escape."

My body goes rigid, absolutely still. I stare at him for a long time, mouth gaping. He stares back, completely serious.

"You...you must be joking..." I finally manage to whisper. But I know he isn't.

"This place is a travesty, a murder house. They can't keep you locked up anymore," he growls. "But you can't do it alone. So I'm here to help you."

I blink several times, taking everything in. "You're here to help me," I repeat. He nods wordlessly so I continue. "So...keeping me awake, making me feel pain...that was all to help me?"

"Yes."

My eyes narrow suspiciously. "How is that going to help me?" I demand.

Soren levels me with a very serious look. "In order to escape, you must learn how to resist. Resist, rebel...anything to keep them from claiming you," he says.

I listen very quietly, feeling his words pass through me like sparks. They do something to my insides. Move them. Churn them. Set them on fire.

"You need to show them that they don't own you," Soren continues. "*You* control this place. Nothing else can force you. Nothing else commands you."

"But staying awake and screaming…how will that do anything?"

"It will show them that you are strong, that you won't give in," Soren replies.

"But even if I do…even if I fight against them…it won't do any good," I argue, hanging my head. "Why should I fight if it won't help me?"

Soren reaches out and grabs my chin. His grip is firm and somehow comforting. His green eyes burn into mine.

"If nothing else, fight just to spite them," he says. Then he smiles and I smile tentatively back. His words fill me with a low-smoldering passion, a sense of rebellion that I haven't truly felt in years. They make me want to laugh but they also make me want to fight.

But my smile fades quickly. I pull my chin from his hand and turn away. "It's not worth it," I mumble. "Even if I fight, I'll never break free."

Soren narrows his eyes. "You will," he says. "I'll help you."

I glare at him. "How can you help me? I don't even think you're real!"

"Does it matter whether or not I'm real if I can help you escape?"

"You can't help me escape!" I shout. "If I try, they'll hurt me. Maybe even kill me."

"Yes, they will," Soren says, nodding. "But if you escape, it will be worth it."

"Worth it if I'm dead?" I mutter.

Soren stands up so quickly it makes me jump. I blink at him and he glares down at me, his lips curling into a snarl.

"You're a coward," he accuses, sounding thoroughly repulsed.

His words cut deep, spilling anger and pain and indignation within me. But I can't deny the truth to them, and I hang my head in shame.

"Without fear, we'd all be monsters," I say. I don't know if I'm trying to defend myself or speak the truth.

"We're all monsters anyway," Soren growls. "But cowards are the worst monsters. Monsters with no prey but themselves."

I look up then, face burning with embarrassment. He's right and I wish he wasn't. I am a coward and a monster.

"Why should I escape then?" I ask morosely.

"Because you were not *born* a coward, that's not who you truly are. You just became that way when they stuck you in here. Listen," Soren says in a quick, urgent voice. He kneels in front of me, placing his hands on my knees. "You are more than this. You have a right to live and be free and I'm going to help you."

I watch him for a long time, mesmerized by those wheat field eyes. Like the first time, I sink in them, letting their waves overtake me. In them I see myself, running through my grandfather's fields in the bright summer sunlight. And I see Trevor.

Trevor. I close my eyes tightly against the pain.

When I open them again, the answer tumbles like a stone from my mouth- sturdy, resolute, unbreakable.

"Alright. What do I need to do?"

Soren grins, showing all his teeth. "That's my girl."

***

For the next few weeks, Soren has me practice what he calls "quiet violence". Mostly it involves staying awake when they give me sedatives or screaming when they give me morphine.

"Quiet violence can be just as effective as blatant violence," Soren said, and I believe him. Doctor Turtle-face and his nurses, and even some of the guards, have started looking at me funny. With curiosity, concern…sometimes even with fear.

After these practice sessions, when the doctors have left and the guards are off patrolling, Soren comes to me with gifts. They are always small, a lot of the time they're food. He'll bring me candies and drinks from my childhood, and once he even brought me a slice of the pumpkin roll my mother used to make.

Sometimes they're not edible, however. He brought me a book that Trevor passed on to me- *Frankenstein*. I was young when I read it, but I loved it all the same. The hard cover has long since fallen from the well-worn book, exposing the cream-colored pages and the cracked spine.

Soren also brought me a necklace that once belonged to my grandmother. The pendant was a delicate thing, a small, silver rose, its petal's edges dusted with red accents. He even brought me a picture Trevor had painted for me, when he was six and I was just a baby.

That was when I finally broke down and asked Soren if he'd been sneaking into my old house. He told me he hadn't but I wasn't sure I believed him.

Then one evening, a face appears in my door's window. My heart grows sick and my stomach seems to shrivel up within me. Kurt's brown eyes seek mine and a vicious grin parts his lips.

Behind me, Soren sets a hand on my shoulder. "Do not be afraid," he growls.

"Don't leave," I whimper, unable to pull my gaze from Kurt's. The sharp click of the lock makes me jump.

"I won't," Soren assures me, glaring at Kurt as he opens the door and steps inside.

Kurt doesn't see Soren. He looks only at me as he approaches, fingers curled around a large syringe.

"Hello, crazy," Kurt sneers. "I got somethin' for ya." I tremble as he comes closer and prepare myself for the fight.

"No. Don't fight him."

I blink, my eyes expanding to the size of saucers. *What do you mean, "don't fight him"?* I demand.

"Quiet violence for now, Ellyn. Trust me."

Before I can reply, Kurt grabs my arm and stretches it out at an uncomfortable angle. I wince but otherwise make no reaction.

"C'mere, ya little bitch," he says, grinning at me.

Something comes over me then. I feel my insides shutting down and my expression becoming neutral, a true poker face. I stare at him without fear or anger, and something close to nervousness flickers in his eyes.

Kurt stabs the needle into my arm and pushes down the plunger. I can feel, distinctly, the liquid as it enters my bloodstream. I shiver a little at the strangeness of it but otherwise remain perfectly still.

"Gonna have fun with you, bitch," Kurt continues, grabbing my chin. His fingers dig painfully into my face; I imagine they'll probably leave bruises. I stare him down without flinching, or even blinking. In the back of my mind, I wonder if this is how Soren feels.

The nervousness from before returns to Kurt's muddy eyes, but this time it settles and expands into something more. A flicker of delight makes my stomach flutter when I recognize fear in his face.

But the delight disappears as his face wavers and twists around the edges. His grip on my chin becomes tighter- steel clamps digging into my flesh. I start to panic, feel my heart start to race within my chest. I am painfully aware of the neon liquid coursing through my veins; with each pump of blood, it's thicker.

A ringing starts in my ears and muffles everything else. I see Kurt's lips move but I don't hear what he says. I feel like I'm underwater.

From the background of stifled sound, I hear it. At first it's just a subtle thrumming, like the sound of my heartbeat in my ears. But steadily it grows, an endless rhythm, until it's pounding like steel mallets against my skull.

The drumline, I think in despair, rolling my eyes away from Kurt's face.

There they are, all in neat rows stretching from one wall to the other. They make a path to the door and back, drumming on their drums, staring with eyes that don't see.

Kurt doesn't seem to notice and my heart nearly explodes from the thought. *How can nobody else hear such infernal noise?*

The sound surrounds me, *becomes* me. I am aware of nothing else until everything in my vision starts to shake. The room becomes blurry from the sudden quaking, but in the rush of sound I can't figure out why. Is it an earthquake? Is the building collapsing?

A moment later, blackness washes over my sight.

***

Warm, pale sunbeams run in through the window and wash the floor with light. I pretend they're the ghosts of streams running down a mountain, pure and crystal clear. I reach out with one hand and touch the light, coasting my fingers over the patch of warmth.

"Ellyn," Soren says softly.

I don't look at him. I stare at the light, wishing I could fill myself with it.

"Ellyn, I brought you something."

I refuse to look up. My whole body aches from the seizure last night- from my head cracking against the tile floor, from my body shaking so hard it nearly tore itself apart, from the drumming that wouldn't stop until long after I'd fallen into unconsciousness.

Soren slides something across the patch of light to me. It's a shoebox, an ordinary brown cardboard box, with a bunch of little holes punched in the top. After a long moment, I pull the box over to me but don't open it. I continue to stare at the sunlight without speaking.

Eventually, Soren sighs. "What do you want me to say, that I'm sorry about yesterday? I'm not," he snaps.

I look up at him, outraged. "You're not sorry? I had a fucking *seizure* because of you!"

"Okay, I'm sorry about that. But you did the right thing. I never said it was going to be easy," he replies. We lapse into silence for a moment. I'm not sure what to say.

Finally, he points to the box. "You going to open that?" he asks.

I glare at him, considering mutiny. But curiosity wins over everything else, and my fingers gently pry open the lid.

A bird peeps up at me, cocking its head to the left and then to the right. Its onyx eyes watch me without blinking. Blindsided, my mouth falls open. The bird trills sweetly in reply, flutters its wings and darts gracefully to the window, where it sits on one of the bars and sings.

I turn to Soren, gaping, and he chuckles at my expression. "Her name is Lily," he says. "She was a prisoner, too. Once."

I glance up at the little bird singing bravely at the sun and something stirs within me. It doesn't look right for her to have to sit in a barred window.

"She was a prisoner?" I repeat.

"Yes. For a selfish old woman who lived in a mansion by herself. She wanted company so she captured this bird when she was very young. Took her right out of her mother's nest," Soren explains. I don't ask how he knows all this. He seems to know everything.

"And you brought her here?" The skepticism in my voice is heavy, bordering on condescension.

"Even in here, she's free of her cage," Soren replies steadily. His green eyes burn into mine and my legs feel strangely weak. "She already learned her lesson. Now it's time for you to learn yours."

"So teach me," I say, trying to sound challenging.

Soren grins. I swallow hard; something in that grin has my stomach churning nervously.

"I intend to," he says and gets to his feet. "Stand."

I blink up at him, startled by his change in tone. "What about Lily?" I ask weakly. "What if they see...?"

"Put her back in the box. She'll be fine there 'till you let her out again. Now stand."

I scramble clumsily to my feet without another word, shoving the box under my bed. Lily continues to chirp, oblivious to both of us.

"Now, I've taught you how to use quiet violence and you've used it quite effectively so far. But now it's time to kick things up a notch," Soren says. I watch his muscles bunch subtly under his clothes, coiling with energy. His expression blazes with ferocity. I'm scared of the wildness in his eyes.

Then, like so many times before, he levels me with a stark, serious stare and says, "It's time I taught you how to fight."

***

It's been a week but it feels like it's been a month. Soren's been working me incredibly hard, pushing me to my limits and then pushing me *past* my limits. The muscles under my skin feel like bruises, every single one of them. But I've also never felt so energized, so exhilarated in my life.

It's like I'm holding so much freedom in my hands that I don't know what to do with it. I feel like I'm walking on the edge of the world, staring down into the abyss, preparing to take flight into the unknown.

Every morning I pull the box out from under my bed and let Lily out. She sings in the window from dawn till dusk while Soren and I train. And every night she comes to sit on my hand and I place her back in her box until the next morning.

One evening, after a particularly hard session, Soren disappears for a few minutes. I don't know where he went- he's just gone- so I sit beneath the window and watch the twilight fade slowly from the sky.

"Here," Soren says, holding out a bottle.

I jump, startled. "Jesus, how do you *do* that?" I demand, taking the bottle curiously.

Soren chuckles, sitting down on the edge of my bed. "Well, I'm not Jesus, but if I were you I wouldn't question him," he says and sips from a bottle of his own.

I throw him a withering glance and then return to inspecting my bottle. "What is this?" I ask. "There's no logo or anything."

"Just drink it. I know you'll like it."

I do as he says, cautiously. The taste that assails my mouth, however, erases all caution. It's like drinking pure nostalgia. My mouth sings with remembrance.

"Cherry-flavored beer," Soren says as I take a deeper swallow.

"My brother and I used to sneak these from my stepmother's fridge!" I exclaim, hovering over a dizzying wave of memories. I raise an eyebrow at Soren. "So you're trying to get me drunk, huh?"

"I'd have to give you quite a lot of these to get you drunk. Not a lot of alcohol." He stops to take a sip, and then adds as an afterthought, "Pussywater."

I gape at him. "It is not, it's fucking delicious!"

"I never said it wasn't. Just pointing out that's it's not a *man's* drink."

I shrug. "Good thing I'm not a man."

Soren smiles. "Yeah. Good thing."

I feel him watching me for a long moment and I begin to feel hot, flushing under my skin. Desperately trying to ignore this, I get up and sit next to him on the bed. His eyes follow every step.

He stares at me and I stare at the floor, kicking my feet idly. The beer is slowly growing warm in my hand but it suddenly doesn't matter.

"Soren…" I finally say, to break the silence.

"Ellyn," Soren replies.

We fall silent for a moment.

Then Soren gently grabs my face and kisses me.

I don't resist or struggle. I sink into the kiss immediately, letting my body melt. Every bone, every muscle, every particle turns to water. I let him own me, mold my lips to his, eyes closed and mouth parted in ecstasy.

Eventually, breaking apart for air, Soren smiles at me. "You look breathless," he says.

"I am," I reply and my heart swells with an overwhelming need. Before I can summon a coherent thought, I add, "I want to drown in you, be overwhelmed by you, and perish."

Soren just grins. "Dramatic," he snorts.

"I am not. It's true!"

"Never said it wasn't," he says. Then he leans in to kiss me again.

***

Another week passes. Soren trains me, and the doctor's visit me less and less. I read *Frankenstein* to Soren and Lily, and he continues to bring me gifts. Mostly it's food, but he did bring me a pen one day.

"To record your thoughts," he said. "Writing is a beautiful outlet."

So I inscribe my thoughts on the walls, near my bed or under the window. One day, lying on the floor on my stomach, feet kicking idly in the air, I pressed the ballpoint pen to the white wall with the intention of writing a poem. Lily sang cheerily in the window above me and warm sunlight lit the whole room with white, powdery brightness.

A poem never came, so instead I just wrote this: *My sweetheart is not terribly sweet (but he is very much my heart).*

Soren got a kick out of that.

For the first time in many years, I feel happy. I am still trapped in this place, still poked and prodded by doctors, still visited by Kurt. There is writing on the wall. There is writing on the wall and a bird in my window and gifts stashed in my mattress.

And there is Soren. No matter what anybody decides to do to me, I always have him. They keep me in this place where there's so much pain and sorrow and so little love. He brings it to me like an offering, a gift. And it's in him that I find my sanity.

I've never been in love. I saw Trevor fall in love with Sandy, and I saw the love my grandpa had for my grandma every day, even though I never met her. I witnessed it from a distance.

I'm in love now. I feel it in my bones. It bubbles in my veins and my chest. It's like the drumline is inside of me, thrumming heavy beats in my heart. I tell Soren this one night and he laughs.

"What's funny?" I ask, leaning slightly away from him. We are lying on our sides in my bed, facing each other. Lily is already asleep in her box beneath us.

"You were always melodramatic," he replies. Then he smiles and brushes a strand of hair from my face. "That's what I love about you."

"Hope that's not the only thing," I mutter, playing with my grandma's rose pendant. After a moment, I frown. "I'm sorry."

Soren blinks in surprise. "For what?"

"You always bring me all these gifts, and they're amazing! I don't have anything to give to you," I say. Tears prick my eyes at the injustice of such a thing.

Soren only laughs. "Silly girl!" he exclaims. "Love isn't defined by *objects*, nor is it defined by physical essence."

He grows quiet and serious, but the smile remains on his face. Keeping his eyes on me, he reaches out and places his hand over my heart.

"It is the *soul* that feels true love, and it is the *soul* that gives it back," he continues.

I stare at him for a heartbeat, stunned. When I finally find my voice, it shakes slightly. "And you say *I'm* melodramatic."

He snorts. "I get it from you, Ellyn." Then he closes his eyes and curls closer to me.

When I open my eyes the next day, Soren's gone. This isn't that unusual; half the time he's there when I wake up and half the time he isn't. Yawning, I stretch myself out of bed and pull out Lily's box. When I open the lid, she stares up at me and chirps.

I furrow my brows, surprised. Usually she flies right to the window. I reach in and stroke my finger down her smooth, feathered head.

"What's up, Lily?" I ask. "Don't you want your perch?"

Lily continues to chirp at me, staring straight into my eyes. My finger slows to a standstill above her head. A chill seeps through me like molasses, slow and thick. There is something urgent about Lily's tweeting today, and instantly I get the distinct feeling that something is going to happen.

"Soren," I whisper. For the first time I start to worry about where he is and why he isn't here. I close the lid over Lily's head and slide the box under my bed.

"Soren!" I call again, louder this time.

Almost simultaneously, the door slams open, making me jump. I turn my head, but before I can see who it is they slam into me from the side. We careen across the room and hit the wall with a force that sends my head reeling. After a moment, Kurt's face spins into view.

I start to fight but he jams something deep into my arm. My eyes fly open wide. *No!* I think, feeling the familiar liquid blending thickly with my blood.

Terror fills me, followed quickly by a deep-burning rage. Letting out a feral shout, I turn on him, sending my knuckles into his cheekbone. There is a sharp, satisfying crack and he cries out in pain. Scrambling hastily to my feet, I kick the heel of my foot against his nose, snapping the cartilage.

Power courses through my body, and every one of Soren's lessons surges to my brain in a wave of blood and heat. I descend upon Kurt, screaming and tearing, just a bundle of bunching muscles and vengeance.

Eventually, he starts to fight back. He catches my left fist as it flies toward his face, then delivers his own punch, a truly stunning blow.

Hot, flaring agony bursts where my nose is supposed to be. Blood vessels and cartilage break. Heat courses down my lips and pools in my mouth like liquid copper. I try to get to my feet, hand pressed against my broken nose.

The drumming hits me at that moment, loud and vengeful, where before I hadn't noticed it because the fight had taken over everything else.

I fall back on my ass, moving my bloodstained hands to my ears to try and block out the noise. I know it's no use. This drumming is a part of me; it will never let me go.

Kurt shoves me onto my bed, but I feel nothing. The room spins and blinks in and out of sight. I watch Kurt limp out of the room in fragments.

I start to convulse, heaving and tumbling within my own body. There's no one to hold me down. Not like they do when they give me morphine.

The seizure rocks me so hard I feel like my bones will snap. My heart smacks against my ribs. My lungs rattle and clench till I can barely breathe. The drumline carries on, oblivious to my agony.

Eventually I drift into unconsciousness. I waver back and forth between dreams and the waking world. Sometimes when I open my eyes I see Kurt, glaring down at me with blazing eyes. Sometimes I see Doctor Turtle-face and his nurses.

Once when I saw him- talking to Kurt, of all people- I heard him say, "...conduct further tests such as this one. Scare them, hurt them, see what they do. There are other patients with looser screws than her. It would be interesting to see..." And then I drifted away again.

Finally, everything is silent. I fall into a deep and dreamless sleep that leaves me blissfully unaware, until I come to a few hours later.

Blinking open my eyes, the first thing I see are Soren's. For a moment I think I'm flying, flying above the field I used to play in as a kid. I stare into the sea of waving grasses wonderingly, searching for myself. Maybe Trevor is there with me, too...

"Ellyn!" Soren barks.

I cock my head to the side. Soren's here, too? Does he see me anywhere in the field of wheat?

Something brushes lightly against the crook of my neck. I giggle and jerk away from the tickling, curling into a tight ball. The sudden movement sends a horrible searing pain throughout my entire body. My teeth clamp together and my eyes shut tight. The wheat field is gone. I know where I am now.

"Ellyn," Soren says again, voice thick with relief. His hand cups my face and I sigh as his lips brush my forehead. "You need to wake up, Ellyn, there's not much time."

I blink and my head pounds. "What do you mean there's not much time? Time for what?" I ask, pressing my knuckles against my forehead to try massaging away the pain.

"Time to escape."

My heart stops momentarily. My fist grows still on my temple. Soren meets my terrified gaze and I see in his eyes that he's not joking.

I get to my feet, and almost immediately fall back into the bed. The pain explodes within me the moment I stand straight and nearly sweeps away my senses. Little black dots dance in front of my vision, making me sway dizzily. Soren took hold of my shoulders and pressed his forehead to mine.

"Stay with me, Ellyn, stay with me," he urges. He holds me steady while the dizziness passes, repeating this mantra, but I wonder why he doesn't just slap me to wake me up.

"Because you're already hurt. Hitting you would probably send you into a coma," he replies. His tone is joking but strained with anxiety.

I narrow my eyes, frowning. "Are you nervous because I'm already hurt, or is there something you're not telling me?" I ask.

Soren blinks at my bluntness. For the first time, I've taken him by surprise.

"Both," he admits after just a heartbeat's hesitation. He places his hand on my shoulder and guides me away from the bed. "Your escape is very close and time is short. There is one more thing I would give you, and one more thing I would ask of you, before we begin."

I take a deep breath and nod obediently. "Okay."

Without another word, Soren pulls something solemnly from his belt. It gleams and winks dangerously at me, making me flinch.

It's a knife. Silver, razor sharp blade. Gold, polished handle.

"Take it," Soren urges me, thrusting the handle into my hand. Slowly, I wrap my fingers around the cool gold and pull it from his.

"Now listen to me, Ellyn," Soren continues, grabbing my face with both hands and kneeling down to meet me at eye level. "Everything I gave you, everything you kept, you must destroy."

Shock hits me hard. It feels exactly like he punched me in the face, and pain sings through my nerve endings as a single twitch shakes my entire body.

"What do you mean-" I start to say but he cuts me off.

"Ellyn, you must!" he shouts. Then he touches one hand to the knife in mine. "Except for that. You keep that until you're safe on the outside. Then you leave it there, got it?"

I shake my head, reeling. "Why?"

A small smile graces Soren's lips but it doesn't touch his eyes. "It's the only way you'll ever be free of this place. You must leave everything behind and start over," he says.

I look over at the box beneath my bed. "What about Lily?" I ask over the lump in my throat.

"Even Lily," Soren murmurs. "You must kill everything about this place."

I start with the inanimate things. They're easier. I rip the pages from *Frankenstein* and watch them float to the floor like broken wings. I bite into the delicate chain of the rose necklace, breaking it in half, and toss it across the room. Screaming, I rip Trevor's picture into little pieces and leave them strewn across the room.

When I get to Lily, I hold her gently in the cup of my hands, murmuring into her forehead. She chirrups at me curiously and nuzzles into my fingers. Tears course down my face and roll like little diamonds down her feathers.

I look up at Soren and he nods. "Kill your demons. Kill your darlings," he says quietly.

I shake my head. "I... I can't..." I stammer.

"You can-"

"*I can't!*" I scream. Lily falls silent in my hands, watching me with onyx eyes. Soren stares at me, waiting for my sobs to die down. For a moment I don't think they will; they keep rising, becoming more hysterical. Eventually I'm able to force the words out.

"I...killed my parents," I say. Soren's expression doesn't change. He probably already knew this but I have to say it anyway. "My dad and my stepmom. Because..."

My throat closes up momentarily. Memory comes rushing back, lit by perfect clarity. The rain pounding down harshly as I stared up at our new country house. The kitchen knife weighing heavily in my hand, little raindrops dewing along its edge. The rage. The rage stewing inside me, barely contained.

My lips curl into a snarl. "Because that bitch killed my brother," I spit. The tears feel like fire now on my cheeks. "She poisoned him and she would have poisoned me, too, if I hadn't stopped her."

In my head I see the unforgiving blade slicing cleanly through my dad's throat, and *her* cowering in the background, grasping desperately at the closet door.

"She wanted you both out of the way," Soren says quietly, startling me. "So she could have your father to herself."

"And his money," I add bitterly. "Grandpa died just after Trevor joined the army and left us all his money. It started to disappear pretty damn quickly and I had my suspicions. But after Trevor came back a few years later, it all became quite clear."

Soren nods. "Your dad spent money on you and Trevor and she didn't like that," he says.

"So she poisoned him," I finish. "The evil bitch poisoned him and made it look like a fucking suicide. A *suicide*!"

Fury at the memory thunders through me. I pace back and forth across my room, kicking torn pages under my feet. Soren and Lily watch me solemnly.

"Trevor was going to have a baby with Sandy," I continue, my voice cracking. "He was going to raise a family. He wouldn't have committed suicide! *That fucking bitch killed him*!"

Soren's arms wrap around me and he cradles me against him. I bury my head in his chest and sob uncontrollably. Lily burrows her head into my hand and chirps morosely.

When the sobs finally die down, leaving me breathless and aching, I look up apologetically. "S-sorry," I murmur weakly. "That's the first time I… willingly thought about it…"

Soren nods. "I know. I'm glad you did. Now you can leave that here, like everything else," he says.

I shake my head. "I don't know if I can," I reply doubtfully.

He just smiles at me. "You can," he says. "I have faith in you." Then he looks very pointedly at the bird in my hands.

Pain rushes through my chest and a fresh sob escapes my lips. Lily looks back at me and blinks. She makes no sound, but her eyes stare very deeply into mine. There is serenity and wisdom in that look, far beyond what a bird should be capable of.

That look calms me. She knows what I have to do and she's ready. A pleasant numbness steals over me, much like it did when I used my newfound quiet violence on Kurt. We stare at each other without blinking, and while she's watching I snap her neck.

It doesn't take much effort. She's small and delicate and goes quickly, snuffed out like a candle under water.

I hold her warm body in my hands for several seconds. Then I set her on the bed and look at Soren. "It's time," I say, with the calm assurance of one who knows the climax of their story is near.

He nods and smiles just slightly. "Yes, it is."

"What would you have me do?"

"Summon the guards. When they open the door, take them out. You're strong enough now; you can do this."

I nod. "Then what?"

"Take their keys and unlock the other doors on this wing." Soren tries to continue but I cut him off.

"Wait a minute! You want me to let out the *other* patients, too?" I exclaim. Doubt ripples through my frame, shedding unease into the situation.

"Ellyn, you know what goes on here. No matter the condition these people must be set free to make their own choices. If they do wrong, they will be sent somewhere else. But a place this corrupt is meant for no one but the people who run it," Soren says sternly.

I bite my lip, remembering some of the faces I've seen through my window or the screams I've heard at night. *Should I really let these people loose on society?*

Then I think of myself. How I was automatically labeled a nut job simply because I'd murdered my parents, believing that they'd killed my brother. And I think of Kurt and Turtle-face and all their experiments. *What if these people are just like me- wounded, frightened? Could I leave them to rot in here?*

I nod again. "Alright. I'll do it."

Soren dips his head. "Good. When you do, lead them in an attack on the staff."

I shrink back, blindsided once more. "*Lead them?*" I repeat. "How?"

Soren smiles grimly. "Use the staff's weapons against them. The morphine, for example," he explains. "Remember the delusions you suffered. How real it felt."

"The drumline," I whisper, picturing their flying drumsticks and unblinking eyes.

"Yes. Remember what I said, Ellyn. Nothing here controls you. *You* control *here*," Soren says.

It takes me a minute to realize that I'm trembling. Everything seems so suddenly real. I clutch at Soren's shoulders, pressing my palms against his chest.

"I want you with me through all of it," I say.

"Of course."

"Through all of it and forever," I insist, moving my hand to his heart. Then I take one of his hands and press it to mine. I meet his gaze, shaky with tears. "Your soul to mine."

He smiles at me gently. "I promise," he murmurs. "I love you."

"I love you, too."

He kisses me, so softly I barely feel the pressure of his lips on mine. Then he pulls away, and his green eyes are distant and resolute.

He points to the door. "Smash the glass," he says.

I do as he says immediately, ignoring the pain in my hand as the shards cut deep. Blood spills down over my arm. I open my mouth and scream as loudly as I can.

Guards rush to the door immediately, shouting angrily. As soon as the door opens I send my fist into the first guard's mouth. His head rushes back and slams into the door. A second guard steps over his limp body and reaches for me, but I swing the knife and slit his throat.

Soren grabs the ring of keys from a guard's belt and throws them to me. Side-by-side, we rush into the hallway.

"They'll be on us soon," he tells me. "Free them quickly."

I rush from door to door, ignoring my saner instincts. Each patient scrambles out, as though waiting for us, and suddenly, as they fill the hall, I become aware of a noise.

I don't see the drummers, but I feel them within me, filling me up with their cacophony. But this time I embrace it, breathe it in, let it strengthen me. I can see from the wildness in the eyes of the others that they hear them, too.

Soren's voice is warm in my ear. "Very good," he says. "Move to the front and lead them to the final door."

I race to the head of the pack, gripping my knife till my knuckles turn white. Soren shadows me step for step.

Up ahead, the final door opens and guards in white uniforms spill into the hall.

I stare at them for an eternity, embracing quiet violence. Behind me, the other patients rumble restlessly but won't cross the invisible line I've drawn. The drumline pounds away at us.

I smile across the distance. Confusion and nervousness shudders through the guards. I see Kurt's face peering out at me. Then I raise my head to the ceiling and scream.

The patients break rank and the guards disappear in their masses like drowning men. Still grinning, I stalk into the fray, whipping my knife at open flesh.

Kurt falls in front of me, bleeding from a cut on his lip and favoring a hideously broken ankle. He looks up and our eyes meet. His mouth parts in terror. Mine curls in a snarl. The poetic justice of it does not escape me.

I cut his throat. I wish I could draw it out but I don't have time. I'm about the race through the door when I realize that Soren isn't with me. I look around, whipping my head from side to side, feeling panic rise within me.

"Soren!" I holler above the din of battle. "Soren!"

"Ellyn."

His voice comes from my right- calm, peaceful, almost amused. I turn, relieved, until I see him.

He looks like a ghost, pale and nearly transparent. I can see the wall through him. My mouth falls open in shock.

My whole world stops for an instant. Even the drumline halts its frantic pounding, and without the frenzied drum beat to put the fire in their bones, the tribe calms momentarily.

"What's happening?" I whisper. I barely make a sound.

Soren smiles at me. "This was always going to be the end, Ellyn. I can't stay with you. Remember? Kill even your darlings," he says.

I'm screaming before he can finish. "*No!*" I shout, tears streaming down my face. "*No, no, no!*"

"Yes," Soren counters. "Yes, Ellyn, yes. Listen! You love me, right?"

I glare at him, but I have no choice. "Yes. I love you. I love you."

"Then do as I say. Go!"

His words break me, but I obey. I race out the door, down another hall, and out through the main doors.

It's raining. The rain pummels me like little fists as I skid to a halt outside what has been my prison for the last three years. I stare at it for a long time until the sobs trickle into hiccups. Then, slowly, I look down at the bloodstained knife in my hand.

A knife imprisoned me. A knife helped me escape. A soft smirk curls my lips, surprising me.

"Melodramatic," I murmur. Then I open my fist and let the knife clatter to the ground.

I stare hard at the sidewalk beneath my feet. The fresh, delectable scent of rain on pavement assails me.

Then I turn on my heel and start walking.

BEST KEPT SECRETS

Sergio Palumbo

The old medical building in the Klyza enclosure was located on a grassy hill about 100 miles north of the town of Colchester in Vermont. It was surrounded by a dense forest that made getting to it fairly difficult. Not many were interested in the region to begin with as it was sparsely populated, and far enough away from the rest of civilization to be virtually forgotten. As a matter of fact, given its location and the peculiar patients who were cared for there, no visitor had been seen coming or going in a very long time.

Overlooking a small stream in the distance, the building itself seemed to be watching the clear, swirling waters cascade down the greenish slope. It was a huge, light gray structure designed in the Victorian Gothic style that resembled a castle. Outside its walls were beautifully elaborate gardens, set-dressings for the casual on-looker. The patients were certainly not encouraged to make use of them; they were, in fact, discouraged in every way possible. The exterior of the building is where the illusion ended. Beyond the imposing wooden doors, the facility had been completely modernized; transforming it into a well-equipped, fully functioning psychiatric hospital that would rival any of its modern-day equivalents.

The original architectural design of the site allowed for sufficient light and ventilation, so the structure itself was not in need of updating. The main section of the ground

133

floor housed the clinical and administrative offices, as well as the meeting rooms. The upper two floors were reserved for operating rooms and staff quarters. But the real poison lay underground on three different levels, where the lodgings for the 'special guests' were located. The lower levels were comprised of reinforced walls; that formed stone arched galleries, and the patient rooms. No larger than ten-foot by ten-foot square, each cell held a single bed, a basin and a commode, and was capable of housing a single patient at a time.

On the first night of admission, new patients received a hot bath, a nourishing meal and a clean bed. But the kindness towards them ended there; continuous constraints, strict rules and painful treatments began from that point on, with no means of escaping either the premises or the cruelty that took place within it.

Walter Hesku seemed a frail and sickly young man; his limbs were bony and thin, while his chestnut eyes seemed to possess a deep tinge of sadness. Only thirty-years-old, with black hair and pale skin, he didn't give the impression of one who enjoyed a sunny day, or appreciated the brilliant rays that lit the reinforced narrow window that overlooked a meadow of flowers outside. At least his room was clean, with its small bed and white walls. This represented the entirety of his tiny world at present. He was housed on the first of the basement levels, and was actually rather fortunate in that regard. The patients living in the lower levels didn't have a window, not even the unbreakable locked variety.

Why did they keep him in here? Hesku wondered incessantly, he was not insane, of this he was absolutely certain. Why couldn't they see that, and why didn't they recognize him as a man of higher than average intelligence? He really didn't understand it. How could he show them he was mentally competent and convince them to free him?

He was deeply convinced that a strange madness reigned over the place. It was the odd, uncompromising insanity of the entire system, and the strangeness of the administration and staff that permeated every aspect of the institute.

The feel of the place was suffocating; a sense of immobility, silence, persistence and self-constraint. The honest truth was that no one cared; nobody paid attention to him or listened to his unending complaints. No one talked to him, but the silent stares and the speechless gestures of the coarse muscular personnel spoke volumes, more than mere words would have if cried out with all their breath.

Until now, all of his attempts at help had proved useless, and every time he tried to speak to a doctor or have a private talk with the director, he was always caught by a nurse and taken back to his locked room where he would remain in isolation for at least 24 hours. Hesku was running out of options, and he was becoming beaten down and frightened of drawing too much attention to himself. He was well aware that he couldn't keep trying the same things, his hopes of catching a doctor's eye and escaping that horrible place once and for all, might soon be at an end.

Hesku was an aspiring writer but hadn't had much luck getting published so far. He had been sure things were just about to turn in his favor when he was seized from his home and effectively imprisoned in this dungeon.

The hospital seemed to specialize in the permanent – *not temporary* – care of those who stayed there. The patients were apparently never meant to be discharged. The place was more like a prison than a medical facility, where empathy, pity and kindness were entirely absent; at least in his experience. At times, Hesku was not only witnessed to, but the victim of such abuse, atrocities that included brutal beatings. There were never visible or serious injuries related to those cruel sessions – the guards knew well how to hide their misconduct – but the humiliation and dejection he suffered left terrible wounds on a man's psyche. Those running the supposed hospital subjected the patients to heinous coercion tactics. They acted as judges, not physicians, and simply stole each individuals will to live away.

As was typical of psychiatric hospitals, a large portion of the population was indigent, much like Hesku, making it easy to control them; to dictate the daily lives of the weak who had little or no family that cared about their wellbeing. The residents of this unfortunate institution had few allies as they were forced through the recesses of a callous medical system. *Why isn't this place regulated by the National Mental Health System?* He often asked himself. He deeply doubted the official channels were even aware of this place since his efforts to reach the director or anyone of a higher authority had been so easily thwarted with deliberate intent. Hesku knew he was in his right mind, and did not need mental care. He knew they were wrong in their assessment of him, and there was no reason to keep him secluded in this place. Unfortunately, his attempts to explain this had proven unfruitful.

The reclusive patient knew his legal rights. According to the law, a physician or other qualified licensed practitioner, as appointed by each state, was required to conduct a face-to-face evaluation with anyone placed in seclusion or restraints for behavioral management within one hour of initiation. But since the day he entered the building, he had not seen a doctor, not even one, only the plump nurses and cruel male personnel who roughed up the patients, controlling them with force. And where were the survey agents who were supposed to check on facilities such as this one? Hesku knew enough about the National

Medical System to know that in order to develop a standardized level of care among the hospitals, and to monitor and stem abuse, this balance in the system was not only vital, but again, required by law.

But Hesku had never seen anyone from an outside agency enter the building and examine the patients to report about their condition, and the overall state of patient care. Unless their visits happened at night or when he was confined to his room – something he genuinely doubted – then no such agents had ever visited this place!

All of it seemed very unusual, strange and out of place. There was no valid explanation for it. But when he mentioned it, the employees unceasingly insisted that he was the unusual one, the strange one; the mad individual who needed seclusion and restraint in order to be kept calm for his own good whenever they deemed it necessary.

There was no way out, no escape from this stricture – night or day. Hesku was well aware of that now. He had learned it clearly over the course of the first two months he spent there. Two months with no valid reason for his imprisonment in such a facility, spending most of his days alone in his small room with no means of communication with anyone in the outside world. No internet access, no phone, no television – not even a radio. *How was it even possible in this day and age to be so cut-off from society?* What could he do to change his impossible situation? He simply didn't know, and that's what made him cry from time to time, waiting willingly, almost longingly, for the nurse to come with her tonic and anti-anxiety medication to ease the pain of thinking and caring about his situation. The isolation is what made him nearly lose hope and welcome the unconscious bliss of ignorance. At least in that condition, Hesku didn't feel the pain of his seclusion, the grief at such unfair treatment, the complete absurdity of his situation. When he was drugged, his mind didn't torture him hour after unending hour with questions about why he was there; why he was forced into this tiny existence away from the world he knew was outside of this building. A world he loved with all its busy streets, shops, towns, woods, parks and beautiful scenery. That was the world he remembered so well. But there were no traces of it here. No connection to the things he had taken for granted in a light-hearted life that seemed so long ago.

He often fantasized of escaping, evading the surveillance cameras, and somehow getting outside the building where he would struggle his way through the woods to the closest town. Perhaps then he could find help, someone who would care enough to assist him evade this lunacy. But the structure was well protected, the close-circuit TV cameras covered every corner of the place as far as he could tell – they probably even monitored his tiny bathroom, he really had no way of knowing for certain. The security was strict and extremely efficient – without a doubt there were a multitude of locked doors, and probably several control stations on the ground floor. Even if he had all the necessary keys, speed and stealth would hardly have made a difference. He knew this in his heart, and he was smart enough to realize that it was the only logical way to keep the patients from escaping. Being caught and thrown into a smaller isolation room that smelled of urine or worse, where the lights were kept blazing 24/7 in the bowels of this abominable place, kept him from allowing those fantasies to become fully fledged thoughts. He forced the mental taste of freedom into the deepest recesses of his mind, where it would remain safely hidden.

One morning, they woke him earlier than usual and led him to a room he'd never seen before. In stark contrast to the bare white he was accustomed to, it was painted in shades of chestnut brown. There was a window in the wall opposite the door, and in the center sat a desk and two chairs, one on either side.

***

After a moment or two, a slim blond-haired, fair-skinned man entered the room. This man was the first physician Hesku had seen since his arrival. Wearing a pair of glasses perched on his thin nose, and an odd expression on his face, the doctor seemed a stern man with deep dark eyes whose silent pupils pierced straight to their subject's soul.

"I'm Doctor Casey Longford." The man began speaking in a hushed tone that made his voice seem even deeper than it really was. "Please, have a seat, Mr. Hesku." His right hand made a sweeping gesture pointing to the chair on the front side of the desk. "I'd like to make something clear. This encounter will only happen once while you stay in this facility," he paused, allowing the information to settle into Hesku's mind.

Still standing, Hesku replied, "What does that mean?" His eyes remained watchful.

"Please, have a seat," the other repeated again. The doctor himself took the seat behind the desk with an air of regal dignity, seemingly staring down at a useless commoner with meaningful intensity.

Hesku did as ordered.

"Again, for the sake of clarification, I'd like you to understand that I realize you are not insane..."

"*What*?" Hesku exclaimed, in a cry that was so high pitched that even he was surprised by its frantic tone. Calming himself, he spoke again, "Can you repeat that, please?"

"Of course, Mr. Hesku. I simply stated that I know you are not insane."

"*Dear Lord*!" the patient burst out with relief. He had been waiting to hear those exact words for a very long time. "You really mean it? You are honestly admitting that I am not insane? I am not mad, I am okay? Why, then am I here? Why am I being imprisoned in this place? Do you know how long I've waited for a consultation with a doctor, to explain my situation and regain my freedom?"

"Mr. Hesku, you will not be speaking with another doctor. As I informed you just a minute ago, this encounter will take place only once while you stay at this facility. This discussion will in no way change your situation."

"What?" Hesku replied, both stunned and angry. The sensation coursing through him was one he imagined a man who had just arrived at the top of a mountain would feel as he discovered that his hands were losing their grip moment by moment, and he would soon plummet from the stony surface. He felt he was going to fall to the muddy and deadly ground further down the cliff. "But you just told me that... What do you mean? I don't understand what you're saying. I don't want you to compensate me for your behavior or for the mistake you made. I am not going to sue you for damages or whatsoever else, I only want to be released from this hospital, once and for all! Please, you know I'm sane. Why keep me in this institution? *What kind of monsters run this building*? *What do you want from me?*"

The physician remained silent, his pupils did not even dilate in response.

Nearly delirious with rage, Hesku was getting ready to stand and wrap his hands around the indifferent neck of this pompous ass when the sight of the doctor's finger resting on the red button on the phone made him stop. He was well aware that a simple tap of that button would bring two muscular men into the room that wouldn't hesitate to beat him senseless. So with a concerted effort, he forced himself to calm down and take control of his rampaging emotions. In a crisp voice, he inquired, "So, why did you bring me here today? Just to tell me that I'm sane? Thank you, but I am fully aware of that. There is no need to explain it to me."

"Actually, that is not why I brought you here this morning, Mr. Hesku," the doctor said. "The nurses brought you before me because I wanted to meet you in person before we proceed further. I wanted you to know why you have been imprisoned here."

'Proceed further?' the thought slammed around Hesku's mind as he grew more and more concerned for his safety.

The doctor began again, "First, I must confess that I personally read your work. The book you wrote…"

"My book? Did you say you read my book…Why? Or better, *how*? It was never published, at least as far as I know. It's only a draft."

"Exactly, and it will never be published, certainly…"

"What?" Hesku stared at him numb with chilling disbelief. "How could you have read it? How did you get the manuscript? How did you even know it existed?"

"I was one of the individuals appointed to check the web that day - the day you sent the manuscript to a publishing house via e-mail."

"Are you one of the editors?" the patient said, looking at him with surprise.

"No, I am not. But I was one of the many appointed employees who check the web each day in search for dangerous texts sent to publishing houses, by authors hoping to be published. In plain English what I'm trying to tell you is that I, and the others of my company, search the web every day for files attached to e-mails. Files that are received by all the editors of every publishing house worldwide, in order to intercept and stop any insidious books from reaching the eyes of the public."

"*What do you mean*?" Hesku exclaimed, incredulous at what he had just heard. "Dangerous texts? What - dangerous to whom?"

"For mankind, surely... What else?"

"Are you actually trying to tell me that you illegally check the e-mail addresses of all known editors associated with publishing companies on the web, and that you, personally, found my book and prevented it from being published for the good of mankind? That's absurd! Why in the name of... *Why would you do that*?"

"Which action are you inquiring about? Our checking the emails, or our choice to intercept your manuscript? First, we check all manuscript submissions, electronic or otherwise. As you are most likely aware, some publishers still will not accept electronic submissions, so we check those the way we always have, by paper mail. It is a tedious task. But since the adoption of the computer age, modern devices and scripted applets save us a good deal of time. Anyway, you asked about your book as well – or manuscript as it is. First of all, I want to congratulate you for having written such a complex and elaborately deep description of the various steps of the process, what did you call it? The *'reincarnation procedure'* as an explanation for the strange behavior of the main character of your story. Your prose evoked a true emotional connection between the reader and the characters in the book, which is why your book was going to become so successful and therefore so insidious as well."

***

"The reincarnation procedure? That's an Urban Fantasy manuscript. What are you talking about, man? I'm no scientist, the manuscript wasn't scientifically based, it wasn't real – it was purely fiction."

The other man simply smiled strangely. "What if I were to tell you it wasn't fictitious?"

The doctor's answer struck him with the power of a blow to the back of the head. *What the hell...* "Are you saying that...? That's not possible, is it? Oh Lord!"

"Actually, in order to make your book more realistic, you wrote a strange explanation for the reincarnation that your main character sensed within himself at a certain point. You took as an example the neutrinos and explained what happens in the center of the sun."

"Yes, I did..." Hesku nodded. His eyes attentive, he listening intently to every word.

"You wrote that all neutrinos are tiny, nearly mass-less particles that travel near the speed of light, and can move as easily through lead as we move through air. But they are notoriously difficult to find. You reported that scientists say they're nearly undetectable, because they have almost no mass and no electronic charge. *'Ghost particles,'* you explained. They're often called 'ghost particles.'"

The patient on the other side of the desk was unable to figure out where the physician was headed with this train of thought, but was more than eager to find out.

"But they are one of space's very important ingredients, and they've played an important role in helping scientists understand some of the most fundamental questions in physics. According to your manuscript, in the 1990's a team of Japanese scientists discovered that neutrinos actually have a smidgen of mass. This tiny bit of mass may explain why almost everything is made up of matter, not antimatter, as a slight asymmetry favored matter over the other. Neutrinos are thought to have something to do with that process..."

Interrupting the blonde-haired man, Hesku interjected, "I really can't imagine why you are telling me this."

"You also wrote that studying neutrinos is a difficult process. They're tough to detect since they interact so weakly with other particles. But science discovered years ago that when the neutrinos interact with atoms, they sometimes give off bursts of energy. As those pass through and interact, they produce charged particles, and the charged particles give off light," the doctor said.

"Exactly."

"You also reported that at the center of the Sun, the temperatures are so high that atomic nuclei can fuse together. As a consequence, on the very rare occasions when some neutrinos interact with one of the atoms, they convert that atom into other atoms."

The patient nodded again.

"You took a rare process that happens in the center of the Sun as the basis for your scientific validation behind your fictional tale. Specifically, you said that neutrinos that usually don't interact with anything at all, will interact with other particles due to very high temperatures and can briefly merge and combine themselves with those, remaining in that state for a while before becoming free once again. You used that scientific process to explain the procedure underlying your manuscript."

***

There was a brief silence in the room.

"Then, you suddenly changed the subject and speak about the human mind, the brain in particular. Human beings, you said, are sentient beings by nature, endowed with personalities that make each of them unique. Following scientific debate you studied elsewhere, most likely, you asked the question that is less commonly asked: *where do these personalities come from?*"

Husku stared at the other man, still bewildered.

"You wrote that personalities are assumed to originate from within the brain as a byproduct of the bio-electrical impulses that make this incredible piece of circuitry function. That makes the personality nothing more than the byproduct of the cells that make up the brain and a reflection of the wider environment that brain finds itself in. But the problem is: where do the individual cells – the cells the brain is composed of – acquire the consciousness that makes personality possible in the first place? You elaborated that clearly there is more to the mind than the cumulative electrical impulses of atoms." The doctor looked across the desk, taking a deep breath before continuing.

"What if the brain is not just a transmitter of personality, but a receiver as well? In other words, just as radios and television sets pick up signals from transmission stations around the world, what if the brain does exactly the same thing by picking up 'personality' signals being broadcast throughout the world, with the unique configuration inherent in each brain determining the resultant personality that one acquires throughout the course of their lifetime? You brought to the table another question: what happens if through this procedure one's personality, or better yet, *one's soul*, leaves his deceased body at the end of a life and enters another? This is what you imagined, isn't it?"

"Yes, yes, it is. But, as you said, all that is only something I borrowed from some speculative and unusual studies. It's a fictitious and unlikely scientific explanation, nothing more, surely. I'm a fiction writer, I told you, not a scientist or researcher."

"But don't you believe it is a possible starting point, or plausible reason, for reincarnation?

"It's only what I imagined for the story, nothing else. It's not what I really believe!"

"One of the characters in your manuscript asked himself another question: does a personality continue to function after the brain has lost the ability to receive signals, essentially after death? Just as the destruction of a radio means the radio waves can no longer be received, it's reasonable to believe that once the brain is destroyed, it too loses the ability to manifest a personality. On the other hand, since the signal itself exists apart from the brain/receiver, there is no reason to assume the product of that 'temporary union' between transmitter and receiver is lost forever. The possibility that it still exists must at least be considered, you concluded."

"Yes, but…"

"In doing so, we may discover that the world of living matter and the afterworld may not be as far apart as many people imagine. Our brains, like radio emitters, launch electronic impulses outward at the time of passing. That energy travels for as long as it needs to, before finding another receptive neural pathway to immerse itself within. It then remains merged with that neural pathway for the time being. As neutrinos can merge with other atoms under exceptional circumstances, the emission and the transfer of a soul from one body to another occurs as a consequence of some incredible energy which is freed at the time of passing. It combines with another mind, due in part to a simple form of cold fusion – different, lower and less strong, but similar in the end – and there it stays, until another death occurs and the process repeats itself again. This is the way you explained the reincarnation of humans, is it not?"

"Yes, but this is all fictitious, as I have said. Something I made up to further the evolution of my story. Some of it is based on excerpts of pseudo-scientific reports; I'll grant you that. But largely mixed together by my imagination, nothing more…"

"Understood. But the detail regarding the procedure, the suppositions, and the overall explanation you provided within your book, though fictitious with slight references to genuine scientific findings, could prove to be a danger. Your book may encourage researchers to explore that premise and perhaps discover *too much*. That's something we cannot allow, at least not for the foreseeable future."

"Are you saying that what I wrote is true? Genuinely true, or simply plausible and problematic? My imagined extrapolations can't possibly be true."

"But it is true," he sneered softly.

"*What*?"

"There have been many people that have made interesting breakthroughs by chance, or rediscovered a process that some scientist from the past has already discovered. But, unfortunately, those people only found again what was meant to remain secret for the time being."

"Secret, you say?"

"For instance, do you remember the patient staying in the room next to yours?"

"Yes, the blonde-haired short man with that big nose… but he never leaves his room."

"He was a promising researcher who one day stumbled upon the process Tesla used in 1935 to move a car using electric transmission from a distance, instead of activating it by direct mechanical means."

"And what does that have to do with me?"

"He did something he would have been better off not doing, Mr.Hesku. There was a reason all the papers Tesla had in his New York hotel room at the time of his death were quickly confiscated by the government in 1943. You see, there are people; I'm speaking of high ranking people, who don't want certain ideas to come to light at the wrong time. There are some advances mankind is not yet ready for, and maybe, it will never be."

"Oh my!"

"I suppose you also remember the man living in the room next to the other patient we just spoke about?"

"Yes, I remember him. He doesn't walk around the building anymore like he used to."

"Because he wrote a very in depth paper, only the draft of what would later become a full thesis, but very detailed nonetheless on the life of werewolves in the forests of Bulgaria."

"What? Stop it! Are you trying to tell me that werewolves are real, too now?"

The man on the opposite side of the desk stared at him for a prolonged period of time before he spoke. "Only madmen really believe that werewolves exist."

"I see…" Hesku said, finally figuring out the point of the conversation, sadly.

"Anyway, his research, even if merely fictional, had to be kept secret. His written text expressed something that couldn't be published for the whole world to read." He stared at Hesku for a moment. "Do you know what Kaczynski wrote long ago? He stated that *'Our society tends to regard as a sickness any mode of thought or behavior that is inconvenient for the system - and this is plausible because when an individual doesn't fit into the system it causes pain to the individual as well as problems for the system. So, the manipulation of an individual, adjusting him to the system, is seen as a cure for a sickness and therefore as good.'* Or so it's been said."

A long silence followed his words. Hesku finally broke that silence, "So, you put all those men in this horrible place as well, stopped their work, destroyed it and put an end to their previous lives because of your paranoia, your hidden agenda?"

"For the good of all mankind at present, Mr. Hesku," the man stated.

"How can you justify all the individuals you've imprisoned in this hospital by force? What explanation do you give the authorities for your conduct? *Unless the authorities themselves are responsible for of all this*, of course…"

"As the infamous statistic claims, one out of every four Americans is suffering from some form of delusion or mental illness. Think of your three best friends: if they're okay, then it's you… It's as simple as that."

Hesku leaned forward angrily. "And, between the two of us, given the fact that I'm clearly not insane, *the one with mental illness must be you!*"

"Good try, but a wasted effort. Knowing you are not mad will not help you prove you're sane in the end," the physician replied coldly.

"Do you know the quote by Guy de Maupassant: *'A sick thought can devour the body more than fever or consumption.'?*"

"A very good quote, Mr. Hesku, but it's of no use. We're holding all the cards, not you. And that simple truth will not change, no matter what you say or do."

"Then what was the point of this visit today? Why even bother telling me all this?"

"Actually, I wanted to meet you in person, to congratulate you on your brilliant text, and your intelligent theory. And I wanted to make sure I told you while you are still sane enough to comprehend what I'm saying."

"After all these months of imprisonment, are you going to kill me?"

"No, we don't function that way. That would attract too much attention; murders are always noticed one way or another. Suspicions can easily arise and frequently force the authorities to investigate further than we'd like. Sooner or later, some policeman could find the evidence he was looking for and figure out something odd is going on, and we can't bribe every officer out there. This way is much safer. We've already filled out a stack of forms and used our contacts to have you imprisoned here for both your own good and the public's safety. You are here indefinitely as a result of a psychological disorder, one that requires routine assistance, and specialized treatment in a controlled environment. As you discovered, you can't escape from this place, but in order to be sure you never attempt to try during the years you are going to be with us – that is the rest of your lifetime – you must become mad, I mean literally insane, but not dangerous. So you will soon undergo a special procedure in order to deprive you of your mental faculties."

"You are the real madmen! The cruel lawbreakers, with hands full of bloody deeds. How can you rationally justify this? What makes you think that nobody will intervene to help me?"

"Everything we do is for your own good, Mr. Hesku. At least, that's what your patient file will reflect, anyway."

"Damn you! You can't bury the truth forever; sooner or later it will come to the surface."

"We'll bury your work along with your mind, forever by the only means we consider appropriate."

"No, you will not! No, don't, *please don't…*"

"Our visit is now concluded. It was a pleasure to have met you in person, Mr. Hasku. Your final treatment will take place at 1800 hours today," that being said, he pressed the red button on the phone next to his waiting hand.

While Hesku was taken away by force and led to his room, struggling in vain to escape the grip of the two bulky security guards escorting him, the doctor thought to himself that it had genuinely been an honor to meet such a man.

The doctor had encountered so many interesting patients over the years, like the man who had rediscovered the long-lost invention of flexible *glass* – dating back to the reign of the Roman Empire – a material that could undermine the value of gold itself, collapsing the global economy. Or that very intelligent boy who had understood the physics underlying the miraculous substance previously created in the 1980s by a former British citizen that could be painted on any surface and provide protection of up to

1000 C. The British Defense Ministry and NASA refused to settle on a specific price for the rights so, when the inventor died and the boy disappeared, nobody successfully found a way to make that paint again. And he could not forget the older woman who had decoded an ancient language carved onto a stone, telling of the actual events that led to the destruction of Atlantis. They had all proved to be very able and clever people. But their mind and their studies had been the reason for their downfall. They had entered a field they would have been better to stay as far away from as possible…

While considering the deep hatred he had seen on Hesku's face, the doctor reminded himself of the old proverb: *Anger is a short madness…*

But thanks to the final treatment he'd be receiving later in the day, the madness, along with the useless desire for freedom, which could prove dangerous, would soon be removed from his mind, once and for all. As a man named W.E. Channing once stated, *'A man might pass for insane who can see things as they are'*…

I DIDN'T KNOW YOU WERE THERE MATRON

D M Smith

Michael stood still and jerked his emaciated shoulders round so he could face Matron. He was careful to keep his eyes looking down at the polished floor. The hem of her starched white apron lay like a ruler against the dark blue of her uniform dress.

"I didn't know you were there, Matron." He spoke fast, trying not to show his surprise at her sudden appearance.

Matron could always find fault, even when you were totally innocent. Matron did not understand innocence; you were guilty if she said you were guilty. Staff began scuttling from their hiding places now that Matron clearly had someone else in her sights.

"Has Nelly McAndrew been taken down to the mortuary yet?" Matron's eyebrows rose to meet the edge of her starched white cap. Its complicated folds and ruffles signalled their own agitation as she spoke.

"No matron, I was just g–" Michael tried rushing his excuse to prevent a violent eruption of her easily-provoked temper.

"Go up to Daffodil Ward. Get a move on, Michael. Now Michael, now. I cannot be kept waiting." Matron continued to sail serenely down the corridor, looking directly ahead. She barely slowed as she spoke; her words trailed after her, an invisible cloud following in her wake.

"Yes Matron. Immediately, Matron. I'll go right away," Michael said to her retreating back, his voice seeming to lose energy like some rundown clockwork mechanism.

Pulling themselves into the corridor's darkest crannies, porters, nurses and cleaners waited, barely daring to breathe, until Matron had passed them by. They remained lurking silently in the shadows until they could be sure she had moved on. As Matron's shadow passed, each one allowed their breath to escape under close control. Matron's vast apron front led the way, while the rest of her corpulent body flowed along the corridor like a galleon under full sail. No one could remember ever hearing her footsteps echo on St Columba's shiny linoleum.

Michael turned back the way he had come and headed for Daffodil Ward. His breath was rasping in his throat by the time he had climbed the staircases to the top floor.

"Why don't you take the lift?" one of the other porters had asked.

How could he tell them the lift reminded him his surgery? Lying strapped to that trolley in the tiny moving space, doors clashing shut, on his way to theatre. Awake. Terrified, yet unable to move a muscle. Matron's face coming close to his own; dropping her shadow across his body and blotting out the light.

Stopping outside Daffodil Ward for a moment, he seemed unwilling to do Matron's bidding. The moment soon passed and once on the ward, Michael slid a skinny hand around the office door. The sleeve of his pewter grey porter's jacket fell back to reveal a bony forearm.

"I've come for Nelly McAndrew," he said from the doorway. Michael looked down at the charge nurse sitting behind a stack of patients' case notes on his desk.

The charge nurse looked up from the pile. His round, ruddy face and neatly pressed trousers seemed at odds with the dingy office and its damp spots on the outside-facing wall. Michael recalled hearing about the new Daffodil charge nurse from the day porters during a morning handover.

"Come up from Manchester," Ted said, while he waited for the kettle in the porter's lodge to boil.

Jonah had sniffed and winked as if 'Manchester' carried some secret. Porters knew everything and everybody, anything of consequence to the world of the asylum. Michael had never understood gossip, though it seemed to fascinate everyone else. Like the tide, people came and people went. He rarely offered up information of his own accord and had stopped asking questions long ago. Answers were something to be avoided.

"Where are you taking Nelly? There's nothing in her notes." The charge nurse looked up at Michael, his crinkled forehead lending his face a puzzled expression.

"To the mortuary."

"What? She's not dead. You must be mistaken." The charge nurse stood and walked over to Michael, who took an abrupt step backwards.

"Oh. Matron said..."

"She's mistaken and so are you. I've just settled Nelly McAndrew for the night. It's Michael, isn't it?"

Michael did not reply and withdrew from the ward office in silence, taking his hand from the doorframe as he turned to go. The charge nurse heard him shuffle down the corridor, Michael's feet occasionally scuffing the linoleum as he went.

In the distance, a sudden cry was cut short. Michael had learned to stop his ears to the asylum's sounds, unless addressed directly. He always ignored cries in the night. The shriek awakened memories he wanted to keep buried. He called to mind a vision of biscuits in the canteen to blot out the unwelcome thoughts. Polly regularly gave him one chocolate cookie and one Garibaldi with his tea after the night shift. Michael would eat half the cookie followed by half the Garibaldi and then repeat the pattern until he had consumed both biscuits, and any scattered crumbs.

In the canteen, hands warming around the thick green tea cup, he smiled his thanks at Polly. Suddenly Polly froze. Michael sensed Matron approaching also. This time he was ready for her and sprang to his feet. He stood up so fast that he almost toppled over, his enormous feet still wedged under the chair. Polly vanished into the dark recess of her kitchen, leaving Michael alone in the canteen.

"Michael, I've just come from the mortuary." Matron's stare drilled into Michael's forehead. "Nelly is not there."

He automatically raised a hand towards his brow. "No Matron. I wa–"

"Where is she, Michael? Where is she?"

"Still on Daffodil Ward, Matron."

Michael screwed his eyes shut as if against a bright light, even though the canteen was mostly in darkness. Matron's bosom heaved. In a rising panic, Michael tried to get his words out quickly to explain the situation.

"She's not dead, Matron. N-n-not dead." Michael's anxiety made him stammer. "No, Matron. The charge

156

nurse said he'd just settled n-n-Nelly for the n-n-night. He sent me away. S-s-sorry, Matron."

"I see."

Matron's eyes flashed momentarily and Michael put his arms up as if to ward off a blow. But she simply sighed and turned on her heel, her large frame gliding silently across the quarry tiled canteen floor. Michael returned to his one-and-a-half biscuits, but the heart had gone from his treat. He sat slumped over the table, toying with the half-eaten chocolate digestive, knocking it gently against the Garibaldi. Polly materialised from the dimly-lit kitchen where she had taken refuge and slid into the seat opposite. She put her hand on Michael's and smiled up into his eyes.

"Never mind, Michael," Polly said.

***

"Polly, Polly, show us your belly. Polly, Polly, getting fat. Polly, Polly, smelly belly." The village children taunted little Polly, joining hands and swirling around her. She had failed to break out of their restraining circle and now crouched on the muddy ground, a dirty bundle of ragged clothing.

"Be off, you bloody monsters," Michael said as he rushed towards the group, alerted by their laughter. He reached out and tried to cuff at least one of the urchins around the head as they made off, still screaming their taunts.

"Oh Michael, what shall I do?" Polly's flushed cheeks were wet from her tears and her short legs were splashed with mud. "They'll put me in the workhouse."

"Father William says you must go to hospital." Polly shrank from Michael as he said the word 'hospital'. "C'mon Polly. It'll be for the best. They say the matron there is very kind. You can't stay here anyhow, not now your mother and father have… have… d-gone."

"Oh Michael, I need you with me." Polly's small body heaved with sobbing as she gradually grew more hysterical. She fought Michael off as he tried to put his arm around her shoulders. Standing with her back to the outhouse wall, she took a deep breath and pulled herself up to her full height. Even so, she would hardly reach Michael's chin. "That hospital… everyone knows it's a madhouse." She hurled the words at him. "You'd see your best friend sent to the madhouse. A child out of wedlock… it's a sin."

"If I could find the man that did this, I'd kill him." Michael pulled up a tuft of grass and twisted it in his hands so hard that it tore in two.

"Oh Michael, he's long gone."

"You're only 13 Polly. You need care. I'll think of something."

"You're like a brother to me Michael. I wish you were. You won't leave me will you?"

"No, my poppet. I'll always be here for you."

Polly began to cry again. "I'll never come out again if I go in there. Not never." She stood up suddenly and ran into the house, her stained and patched apron tossing side-to-side with her body's movement.

***

"Well doctor," Matron said, sipping tea from a tiny china cup. She looked up and fluttered her lashes over its rim. "Of course you are quite right. The child needs care and should stay under lock and key… for her own safety. Obviously she cannot be left unsupervised. I will see to her care… personally."

"Matron, you are such a saint," Doctor Tevis said, smoothing his cravat with long manicured fingers. "We are so lucky to have you with us here."

"Oh Doctor Tevis, it is nothing. Any caring person would do the same... for one so... so young" Matron reached into her vast apron and pulled out the smallest, finest of lace-edged handkerchiefs. She dabbed at the drool that crept from the corners of her mouth and threatened to drip on her vast bosom.

"It is strange, of course..." said Tevis reaching for another biscuit so that he could look away. "Strange that the lad who brought her in is quite mad too. Such a coincidence. If he were related, a brother say, I would conclude madness runs in the family. I believe the Lancet has reported the occurrence on more than one occasion."

"Oh, Doctor Tevis... you are so learned. You make me feel quite inadequate."

Tevis flashed his finest white smile. "The best thing, Matron, is to keep them separated. Place the girl with the female lunatics and put the lad on a male ward. Medication and surgery... effective treatment... that will be their very saving. Interesting cases, both of them. How fortunate for us to have them here at the same time... and so fortunate for them too. They should be glad that you have taken them in."

Matron escorted Tevis from her office, walking close to him until they reached the grand archway over the main door.

"Please Matron, do not trouble yourself to come further," Tevis said, taking her hand in his and giving it a slight squeeze. "The weather is turning inclement. It would not do for you to risk taking a chill in this cold breeze."

"You are so thoughtful Doctor. Well, perhaps I should go in now. I will call on the lad and the young girl directly and see they are settled in their wards."

Matron closed the door on Tevis with a slight smile on her lips. She rested her head on the heavy oak door for a moment and heard it close with a satisfying click.

***

After his regular ward round, Tevis reported how well Michael had been responding to treatment.

"So docile," Tevis said.

Matron saw how malleable Michael would become. He only needed a little direction. Soon. Soon. She swiveled gently back and forth on the wooden office chair, stroking her hair with one hand. The sound of running feet on the tiled hall floor outside the office interrupted her reverie. A rapid succession of knocks on her door quickly followed the footsteps.

"En–" Matron's instructions were cut short.

"Matron, I'm so sorry to rush… but you said… you said." The diminutive porter opened the door and stood hopping from foot to foot and wringing his gnarled hands.

"Yes, yes, get on with it. Spit it out Stephen. Spit it out."

"Oh Matron. It's the baby… the baby… baby. Her baby. It's… it's… co–"

Matron almost bowled Stephen over in a headlong dash. As she sped along the corridor, she called back over her shoulder. "Follow me. But wait outside the room."

On the ward, Polly's labour was already well underway.

"An easy birth, Matron." Tevis looked up from between Polly's knees as Matron entered the room. "These young girls hardly feel a thing. Just pop it out like bread rolls from an oven."

He began to laugh at his own joke. As if to contradict his words, Polly let out a prolonged scream. The baby slid into Tevis's waiting hands and lay glistening in the light from a naked overhead bulb.

"Give me the infant doctor," said Matron, her eyes staring wide as she reached to snatch the child. Tevis jerked backwards involuntarily as she lunged at him. She stopped herself mid-grab. "Oh doctor. Silly me, so anxious about the child. Such a dear little thing," Matron cooed.

"Of course, Matron. Here, take the tiny mite. A boy." Tevis wrapped a towel around the new-born and thrust the small bundle at Matron.

"So plump," Matron said, unwrapping the baby to inspect it. She seemed unable to restrain herself from pinching his little legs, which made the child shriek in pain.

"My baby… my baby." Polly cried out and struggled to get up. But the leather restraining straps held her wrists firmly. "Give me my baby." She stretched her body as far as she could toward Matron, while her mouth gaped wide in terror.

"I'll give her this to settle her down," said Tevis as he reached for the glass hypodermic syringe.

Stephen lounged on the wall outside Polly's room, but snapped to attention once Matron appeared through the doorway.

"Fetch me the other new admission. He's called Michael. Bring him to me tomorrow morning. Early, before breakfast. Tell no one Stephen. No one." Matron carried off the bawling infant wrapped in its bloody towel. She did not wait for him to be bathed, so great was her rush to claim him.

Next morning, Matron sat in her office chair looking like a fat baby after its bottle. She hummed a gay tune and dabbed at her full, red lips with a handkerchief. There was a gentle tap at the office door. Stephen entered with Michael in tow.

"Bring him in Stephen. There… stand him there." Matron pointed to a spot in front of her desk. "Now go. Wait in the hallway."

Stephen ushered Michael into Matron's office and directed him to stand where she had indicated. Sunlight streamed through the windows and shone on Michael's shaved scalp as he stepped forward. He continued to look down at the floor as if afraid to raise his head and look directly at the woman on the other side of the desk.

"Michael," Matron said as she stood up. Michael remained still. "Michael. You may look at me."

Wide brown leather straps constrained Michael's hands behind his back. But he managed to look up and swivel his whole body around to face Matron. She moved around the desk to stand in front of him.

"I know what you did, Michael."

He continued to stare at her in silence.

"You may speak to me, Michael."

"I d-d-don't know what you mean, Matron. I'm s-s-sorry."

"The baby, Michael. The baby."

"N-n-no, Matron. I d-d-d-."

"You want to stay with Polly, don't you Michael?"

"Oh yes, Matron. Yes, I do." The colour rose in Michael's cheeks, making him look almost handsome despite his shaved head.

"I could send you away... to prison. What *you* did... wicked." Matron spat the words. "What *she* did... sinful."

No sooner had the colour returned to his cheeks than the blood immediately drained away, leaving them pinched and sunken. Michael suddenly became haggard and hunched. Matron came close and stared into his eyes, but he could not hold her gaze and glanced away.

"But you could help her Michael."

Michael's head jerked up at her words. "What? What must I do? Tell me... please."

"Help her, Michael." Matron let the silence hang. "Help her, Michael... and help me too. What you did, Michael." He flinched as she spoke. "Don't be afraid, Michael," she continued in a soft voice. "Don't be afraid... I know, I know." Matron put her arm around his muscular young torso. "I can understand that you want to keep young Polly close to you."

Michael's shoulders began to shake as a sob escaped from deep in his body. His eyes swam with unshed tears.

"You love her don't you, Michael?"

Michael nodded silently and his face glistened in the sunlight as his tears flowed freely.

"You could... do that again... for me, Michael. For me."

Her words took a moment to penetrate the fog in his mind. He already knew the drugs must be affecting him. He felt constantly afraid and his thoughts came slower than before. Matron was out to trap him in some way, or perhaps he had misunderstood her?

"The baby?" he asked, raising his head to look at Matron. "Polly's baby. What happened to her baby?"

"You need not worry about it Michael. I've taken good care of the baby. You won't see it again. It's gone... gone."

He continued to look at her, his eyes wide. His growing anxiety made him forget his tears. There was something he could not quite grasp in her words, some hidden significance in what she had said. *What did she mean?*

"And if there were to be more... babies... babies... for me... for me... Michael, you could forget them too. Now Michael, what do you say?"

He had no choice. "Yes Matron," he whispered, still fighting the mist that confounded his thinking. He shook his head as if to clear his thoughts. "Yes" seemed to be the word she was expecting.

"What Michael? I didn't hear you. Speak up." Matron had left soft words behind. Her voice was becoming increasingly strident.

"Yes Matron," Michael said, summoning all his strength to look her directly in the eye. The shock of contact made him drop his gaze as if her eyes had burned him.

"Good boy, Michael... good boy... sensible boy." Her soft voice had returned. He liked this voice even if he did not understand her meaning. There was something, some shadow. But as his mind reached for it, the shadow submerged beneath the other shapes swirling inside his head.

Matron opened the office door and called out to Stephen, "Take him back to the ward now Stephen."

***

Michael looked up at the clock on the high central tower. Thirty minutes until his shift ended; time to visit Daffodil Ward again. But first he must fetch a trolley. This time he would take Nelly McAndrew to the mortuary. On the ward, Michael watched as the charge nurse stood over a bed at the far end. Becoming aware of an observer, the charge nurse looked up. As he reached Michael, he ushered the porter into his office.

"How did you know?" the charge nurse asked. Michael simply stared back, his rheumy eyes unblinking. "So full of life one minute... and stone dead the next. Nelly was so full of laughter. She loved her food... so plump and rosy. How did she die? I don't understand it. There was no sign." The charge nurse began to pace around the office. "What's going on?"

"Just doing my job," Michael said. "Been sent to collect Nelly McAndrew. Take her to the mortuary. 'Immediately,' she said."

The charge nurse watched dumbfounded as Michael backed out of his office to wheel a squealing trolley up the ward. Other patients were still drinking their early morning tea. Some pulled their faces in an ugly grimace as he passed their beds, some rocked to and fro and hugged themselves. One waved her arms in a huge semi-circle. Michael ignored the women and began to haul Nelly's body off the bed. Horrified, the charge nurse dashed up to stop him.

"Put her down this instant." The charge nurse pulled the curtains around Nelly's bed. "Have some decency man. She's still warm."

"Matron said to fetch her straight away," Michael said, picking up the body once more. He cradled Nelly in his arms and looked down at her yellowing waxy skin, remembering her plump, rosy cheeks. He took extra care as he laid her body on the trolley and covered her with a white sheet. Pushing gently past the charge nurse, Michael wheeled the trolley between the beds and off the ward.

"I'm going to find out what's going on here," the charge nurse shouted after him. "You just see if I don't."

Once the trolley's squealing had receded down the corridor, the charge nurse slipped off the ward to follow Michael. The porter turned around twice as he manoeuvred the still squealing trolley down the long sloping corridor leading to the mortuary. Built below ground level, the corridor was dimly lit by a few high windows that let in the early sun's slanting rays. Each time Michael turned, the charge nurse slipped quickly into the shadows. Michael continued his journey, aware of a follower but unable to see who it was. Eventually, the rubber doors of the mortuary flapped shut to swallow Michael, the trolley and Nelly's corpse.

Rushing forward, the charge nurse soon reached the black rubber doors. He pulled one carefully open and stepped through into a small vestibule. On the other side stood a second set of doors and beyond that, the mortuary. Looking through a high round window in the mortuary door, he spied Michael and Matron speaking to each other across Nelly's inert body lying on the trolley. Matron said something inaudible and pulled back the sheet covering Nelly's face. Michael stood looking down at the corpse, as if to pay his last respects. His large hands hung limp at his sides and his long, skinny arms dangled loose inside the sleeves of his grey jacket. He turned and made as if to exit the mortuary through the vestibule where the charge nurse was still in hiding, but paused and seemed to change his

166

mind. He said something to Matron and left through a small door in the far corner of the room.

The charge nurse waited to see what would happen. Matron reached into a drawer and took out an all-encompassing, pristine, starched white coat and put it on over her uniform. She walked to the instrument table and slowly selected several shining implements. She carried them back to the trolley and placed them on a polished steel side table. The charge nurse stood on tip-toe to observe her actions through the window.

But Matron walked round to the near-side of the trolley and now stood between him and Nelly's body. With her back to the charge nurse, Matron had blocked his view. All he could see were her arms and hands moving swiftly over Nelly's body. Matron wore no gloves and her hands were soon running red. She seemed to keep touching her face, but the charge nurse could not make out she was doing. Her actions made no sense. Eventually he could contain his curiosity no longer. He threw open the door and strode into the mortuary.

"I don't know what you think you're doing, Matron," he said as he crossed the floor to stand at her side. "But I don't like the way things are being handled here."

Matron swung her bulk round to face him. She looked like a naughty child suddenly caught in the guilty act of holding a fresh-baked cherry pie. Her lips had grown plump and ran with delicious red juices. She dropped what she had been holding and wiped the back of her hand across her face. The action smeared red wetness all the way across one cheek to reach her ear.

***

"Oh Doctor Tevis, I'm so glad you could come out at such short notice." Matron hovered around Tevis, relieving him of his overcoat. "And on a Sunday too. I do hope I have not interrupted your golf?"

"Good Lord, Matron. Your needs are far more important than my golfing Sunday."

"I suppose there will need to be an inquest?"

"Oh don't worry about that Matron. The coroner is an old university friend of mine. It is clearly an open and shut case. The charge nurse obviously had an underlying cardiac condition. It was only a matter of time before a heart attack carried him off. He was slightly overweight too you know." Tevis reddened. "I don't mean... you know... he... I mean, looked unfit."

Matron rushed in to cover the doctor's embarrassment. "He must have been trying to help out by pushing poor Nelly McAndrew's body down to the mortuary. It was such a rusty old trolley. And such a long way from Daffodil Ward to the mortuary too. The exertion... it must have..."

"So distressing for you, Matron. I believe he had not been with you all that long?"

"No. Only recently arrived from Manchester. Of course, he never seemed well, but I took a liking to him. I felt sorry for him and wanted to give him a job. It seemed a shame... being so unwell I mean."

"You are an angel, Matron. Always wanting to look after other people."

Matron giggled like a school girl. "That must be the reason I went into nursing. It is my life's calling you know doctor."

"Any family?"

"What?"

"The deceased... your charge nurse."

"No. Oh no, no one. He told me his sad story at the interview. I think that is also why I took him on in the end. Such a pleasant man, but so lonely."

"And Nelly McAndrew? Will there be any mourners?"

"No. Such a pity. No one will be coming for her funeral. You know how it is with our patients doctor... they are the world's cast-offs, the world's unloved and forgotten people."

"It is just as well that you are here then Matron, loving them as if they were your own family."

"True, true, doctor. So many lonely people have passed through my hands." A tear squeezed out of the corner of her eye. Matron dabbed it away with the tiniest, daintiest of white lace handkerchiefs.

INTERVIEW WITH A PATIENT - #0494772

Delphine Boswell

Monday, December 21

"So, can you tell me, Damien, what exactly happened on the night of October 28?"

The man in the wheelchair grasped the vinyl arm rests, the veins on his hands rigid and purple. "When the police asked, I told them it wasn't my idea; it was Miles's. Miles told me I shouldn't have to take the blame."

"Go on," I said, scratching the name Miles into the notebook on my lap.

"I was looking out the eighth-floor window. A light drizzle was falling. The asphalt appeared more like a mirror than a road, reflections from street lights, headlights, and the gold glow shining from the windows of Eloise Mental Hospital." Damien chuckled. "...known around these parts as the crazy house." He stopped and looked at me from the side of his eye. "Tanya, have you ever been in a crazy house before?"

I didn't answer.

Damien closed his eyes and began to rock ever so slightly in his chair. "As a kid, I loved the smell of rain," he reminisced. "The freshness reminded me of my grandma's newly washed sheets that hung on the line to dry for most of the day."

"Ah, yes," I said, noting the man's ability to quickly change topics. "Can you tell me what else you remember from that night—October 28?" In my schooling at Argonaut University, where I was in my third year, working toward a doctorate in psychology, my professors had often addressed the mental patient's natural ability to drift off into their own thoughts, their own worlds. I had been told it would be my job to keep patient #0494772 on track, on task, yet to enter his mind and to see life from his perspective.

With his eyes squinted and his tongue moistening his lips, Damien went on. "People, people without umbrellas... their heads covered with everything from newspapers to briefcases rushed from their parked cars or the city bus, which had just stopped on the corner of Brent and 8th Avenue. Like a colony of ants, they hurried up the concrete steps. That's when I spotted her." His eyes glistened, and his nails tapped rapidly on the arms of his wheelchair.

"Who, Damien?" I jotted down that I sensed a sudden excitement in his behavior; no maybe a better word was anxiety.

Ignoring my question, the patient went on. "...probably visitors, I suspect. Stupid enough to think they had time to make it up on the ward to see their relatives and friends. Others, probably care givers and staff, who planned to clock in before eight o'clock."

More backtracking, moving away from the question at hand, I wrote.

He paused for a moment before going on, and then with his eyebrows raised, he said, "Margaret... it was Margaret who I saw."

On October 29, the newspaper headlines had read:
Head Nurse at Eloise Mental Hospital Found Stabbed to Death

Damien's expression resembled that of a child who had been given a double-scoop of ice cream. He rubbed his hands together, a slight oozing of saliva ran down his chin, which he caught in his hand and wiped in his pants.

Purposely acting ignorant, I said, "Damien, who is Margaret?"

"Margaret?"

Could it be that he had already lost track of our conversation?

"Yes, you mentioned a Margaret. You saw her that night crossing the street to the hospital."

"Oh, Margaret. She's the head nurse in charge of the E.S. ward."

E.S., yes the newspaper article had indicated that Margaret Sullivan had headed up the Electric Shock Department at the institution. She had been a mainstay at the hospital for over twenty-five years, and everyone at Eloise was shocked to think that a woman who was known for her kindness could have been so brutally murdered. That was part of the reason why I had been sent by the university to interview the psychotic man. Once I had gathered the so-called facts directly from the patient, I was to prepare a presentation to the Neuro-Psych Department at

Argonaut. The account of the murder was to be given from the perspective of what I had been told was a man with a near MENSA IQ, who had been diagnosed as a paranoid schizophrenic, type 295.30, according to the pages of the *Diagnostic and Statistical Manual of Medical Disorders.* Other than that, I knew nothing else about him. I needed to learn about his history, and why Electric Shock was going to be considered as a last resort for the patient.

Tuesday, December 22

When I arrived at Eloise, I found Damien in his usual place, staring out the same window he had been the last time I visited. I tried to position my chair so that I could look face-on with him as opposed to sitting at an angle from him, but he released the brake on his wheelchair and rolled slightly ahead of me. I would just have to make do; I certainly didn't want to upset the man. "Damien," I said, "could you tell me how you ended up at Eloise?"

He laughed quietly to himself, began to hum a Country Western tune, while his long fingers kept beat with the melody.

I repeated my question.

He looked at me as if seeing a stranger. "Who are you?"

"Damien, you remember. My name's Tanya Morris. I'm a student at Argonaut University. We spoke yesterday."

He cocked his head to the side until the veins in his neck went taut.

"What are you doing here?" his face confused.

"I'm interested in you, Damien. I want to learn more about you."

Without any more prompting, he picked-up the conversation as if it had never been diverted. "Been here nine years. It was Miles who actually got me committed."

Miles, the name was coming up again.

"How so?" I asked.

"I used to be a professor. Did you know that?" he asked.

From what I had been told about his IQ, it did not surprise me.

"University of Elkwood. I'd gain tenure and all. Taught chemistry."

"Did something happen there?"

This time the man laughed out loud, so boisterously that three patients playing Yahtzee nearby stopped and stared. Like children, they put their index fingers across their lips and said, "Shh."

"You were saying that you taught chemistry at the University of Elkwood."

"Jon Fennemore, yeah, that was his name. An arrogant son-of-a-bitch. I invited him to the lab." Damien looked over his right shoulder. "What's that?"

"Tell her. Tell her it was my idea, Damien."

"What was that you said, Damien, about an idea?"

"Not mine... Miles had an idea. He told me exactly what chemical to put in the test- tube." Damien smiled, revealing a perfect set of aligned teeth. "I watched the mixture warming and rising. I called Fennemore to come over to get a closer look. Then, I tossed the liquid in his face." Damien's head nodded.

I jotted down that Damien appeared smug. His expression definitely spoke of self-satisfaction, almost a pride in what he had accomplished.

"What happened to the student?" I asked, almost afraid of the upcoming answer.

"Scalded his flesh, lost sight in both eyes, dropped out of Elkwood."

"And you? What happened to you?"

"Some shit-head psychiatrist gave me a battery of tests. Said it was evident I was a genius, but due to the voice I kept hearing, he said I was not safe to walk the streets." Damien tugged on the corner of his lip. "To this day, Miles is convinced I did the right thing."

"And you? What do you believe Damien?"

He released the brake on his chair and abruptly rolled back and swung sideways so that he was looking me directly in the eye. "I always do what Miles says, wouldn't you?"

The stern expression on his face and the way he slid back in his chair gave me a sudden chill. It was obvious that Damien did not want me to say anything against Miles.

"How long ago was that?"

"Nine years almost to the day."

Wednesday, December 23

I wondered what one would do with their time as a patient in the Eloise Mental Hospital. I chose to return to the very point where Damien and I had left off at yesterday.

"Nine years... that is a long time. Could tell me what you do here? Damien, how you spend your days?"

"I'm lucky to get outside... short walks in the garden twice a week, always escorted by one of the care givers, and never on rainy days. Rainy days are my favorite."

"So you had told me," I said.

"I'm told I'm a flight risk; though, I've never tried to escape this damn place." Damien cocked his head to the right.

"I keep telling you I've got the perfect plan. Go down the clothes' chute to the laundry. Remove the..."

Damien threw his hands up and covered his ears. His head violently shook sideways.

"Is Miles telling you something you don't want to hear, Damien? Tell me more about this plan of his." I turned slightly to the right.

The man let his hands fall limply into his lap, looked at me and smiled innocently.

"Besides your walks, what other kinds of things do you do here?"

"Most days I sit right here in the parlor. I stare at the wall or my feet or out the window. Some of these guys," he said, throwing his arm out and motioning to two men sitting at a table, "enjoy playing checkers. Others watch that TV," he said, pointing to a small shelf in the corner, the set on mute. "Once I asked one of the nurses why the volume wasn't on. She said we, patients, were not to be stimulated by the sound. Can you believe that bullshit?"

"Tell the lady about the dance I taught you, Damien."

This time I was certain; this was no whisper. I heard the voice with my own ears, gravelly, compelling.

"Okay, okay. Sometimes, Miles tells me to dance, so I tap my black leather shoes on the vinyl floor and listen to the beat. Country, yeah, that's my favorite."

I noticed the patient had no laces in his shoes. He caught me looking at them.

"No one is allowed to have laces in their shoes anymore ever since one of the patients on Ward D tied several pairs together and made a noose for his neck."

"How awful!"

"Not really. Least he earned his way out of this place."

I wrote down *matter-of-factly*. Yes, that's how Damien seemed to approach life. Maybe, it made it easier for him to accept life as he had come to know it. I thought I would shift gears and ask Damien a more personal question. "How old were you Damien when you first heard Miles speaking to you?"

"About twenty-four when I realized that I was hearing someone. No one else seemed to be aware. At first, I thought Miles was nothing more than a small devil, who sat on my left shoulder and encouraged me to do bad things. The nuns at St. Michael's Elementary had told us third-graders at the time, that an angel sat on our right shoulder and a devil on our left."

I listened with interest to his explanation. The nuns had told me the same story when I was a child.

"Our conscience was left with making a choice. If we listened to the angel, we acted on virtue, and if we listened to the devil, we sinned."

"So you thought Miles was the devil?"

"At first, I did. My mother even took me to Rome... a Father Bruno, known for his work with Satan, tried to rid me of the voice."

"You were exorcised?"

"I guess that's what they called it. It didn't work."

"Then what?"

"Mother started taking me to a string of doctors. Some claimed I needed more rest; that I had an over-active imagination. It wasn't until years later, after the incident in the lab, that I got the label that officially gave me a place in this joint. Even after nine years of attempts by the staff to rid me of Mile's voice, I still hear him."

Definitely a paranoid schizophrenic I scribbled, closed my notebook, and left.

Thursday, December 24

"What kinds of things has the staff done to try to help you?" I asked Damien.

"On Mondays, I go for what they call around here as state-of-the-art treatment.   One time, it might be hydrotherapy."

I must have appeared confused.

"Two attendants help me into a large, porcelain tub."

"I told you to fight the fuckin' guys off; they're perverts; that's what they are!"

"Were these guys perverts, Damien? Why didn't you fight them off?"

"I have to admit being totally in the buff in front of two males hasn't really appealed to me. I've gotten used to the baths, though. Water shoots out from spouts in the tub. It relaxes my stiff muscles."

"It must be tough sitting in a wheelchair for hours at a time."

He went on. "Tuesdays, I'm taken to this small room, painted a light yellow. No windows, only a small, barred viewing glass at the top of the metal door. I sit in a red vinyl chair. One of the attendants puts a black hood over my head. Doctor Holmes ordered this treatment for me when I first came to Eloise. Been going ever since."

"What's the purpose?"

"Supposed to deprive me of any sensory input. Was told by sitting in isolation, it would diminish Miles's voice, but Miles doesn't give-up that easily. I tried to tell the good doctor this. Even tried to introduce him to Miles, but Miles refused to speak."

"Why should I have? The guy's a prick; that's what he is."

I sensed now what it was like to be persecuted by an inner voice. All I could conclude is that it would drive one mad; it would have to. I studied the man before me. Here sat a relatively handsome man, in his late thirties, dressed in a pair of jeans and a blue oxford shirt, his hair buzzed like a sailor fresh off a destroyer. If it hadn't been for the wheelchair or his obvious location, if I had just bumped into him on the street or been approached by him in some small café, I would never have guessed that inside this individual lived a tormenting demon. It needled his sanity, played on his emotional well-being, and refused to remove its clutches from an otherwise brilliant mind. So sad, so tragic, I thought.

"Sounds as if you're kept quite busy here, receiving treatments and all."

"Mid-week, one of the nurses takes me to the needle cabinet. I'm locked in a metal cabinet."

"Really?" I wondered if this could be true... a needle cabinet.

"Pressurized water pours over me. No one has ever explained the purpose of the needle cabinet, but I assume, it's just more of the same... to rid me of Miles."

"Never!"

Thank goodness Miles remained. He was, after all, the voice of reason, I thought.

"If you don't mind, Damien, let's get back to Margaret and that night. She was in charge of the Electric Shock Department, so I understand. Were you afraid Margaret was going to try and shock you?"

His shoulders stiffened and pulled back. A scarlet haze came over his face. He rubbed the bristles on the sides of his cheeks, the noise like scratching on sandpaper. "No, anything but that, I screamed, but they wouldn't listen."

"They? You mean Margaret?"

"Nor the doctors. I had seen with my own eyes what the E.S. treatment did to these people. Wipes away their memories, turns them into some kind of zombies. They no longer walk upright but sit crumpled and contorted in wheelchairs lined up along the walls. Their heads, lie on their chests, and bob ever so slightly. Sometimes, I hear them humming, nothingness tunes, over-and-over again."

I listened intently as what the man described to me sounded more like a horrible nightmare, something that one would wake up screaming from.

"One elderly woman yanked on the fine strands of her hair until she was nearly bald."

Damien reached his hand out toward me, and I immediately recoiled. Students at Argonaut were given strict instructions never to let a patient get within three inches of us and, certainly, not let a patient attempt to touch us.

"Did I frighten you, Tanya? I only wanted to demonstrate how the woman toyed with her hair until every last piece was pulled out."

I swallowed hard and pretended to regain my composure.

"A guy plucked at his beard, his fingers working like tweezers, until small droplets of blood covered his bare chin."

"How awful." Suddenly, I began to realize that the picture Damien had painted about the after effects of the electric shock treatments had to be the truth as it was too horrendous to be otherwise, complete to his morbid details.

"And that's why... why you killed Margaret... to avoid having to go for E.S?" The words slipped off my tongue like a spoon of whipped cream, smooth and without friction.

"Margaret deserved to die."

"Is there any question?"

I sat on the edge of my seat. I couldn't wait to hear Mile's rationalization for murder.

"Miles kept asking me, 'Is this what you have in mind for yourself? Are you going to allow this to be your fate?' He was right, of course. If I had refused the treatment, I would have been put in a straightjacket and shackles and locked away in a padded cell." The lines or

Damien's forehead deepened like cracks in a porcelain statue. "That's when Miles came up with the plan."

"Tell the lady my idea, Damien. Go ahead. Tell her."

"Yes, tell me, please."

"For a few days, I'd been eyeing another patient's room... Eli Benson. The guy's deaf and mute. I snuck into his room when I was sure he had left for one of his therapy sessions."

"The doors aren't locked?" I asked.

"Patient rooms are required to remain open at all times. I quickly tore off my clothes and slipped into Eli's. I even had made myself a fake moustache during craft classes and positioned it on my upper lip, just like Eli's. I was lucky enough to find one of Eli's ID tags and pinned it to my shirt... er Eli's shirt."

"You're one cool dude, Damien."

I smiled to myself.

"I failed to mention that a few days before all of this, I did what Miles suggested. I broke one of the spokes from my wheelchair. My fingers had blistered and bled as I twisted and turned the spoke, forcing it to snap, but I knew the outcome would make it all worthwhile."

I looked down at the left wheel on Damien's chair. Sure enough, one of the spokes was missing, and upon closer observation, I could see the dried sores, bloody scabs, on the tips of his fingers.

"Weren't you afraid... afraid of being caught?"

"I had no choice. The night I sat and looked out this very window, I spotted Margaret. Dressed in her white nurse's uniform, she was easy to find, even on a rainy night. I gave her some time to take the elevator to the eighth floor, get situated in her nurse's station."

A sly smile came over Damien's lips. He appeared crazed, mad, insane, and every bit the part of his diagnosis: psychotic schizophrenic.

"You see, I really didn't have a choice." He looked at me as if waiting for validation, as if I were about to nod in approval. When I didn't, he said, "You do see, don't you?" His voice rose, his hands in fists upon his lap.

I looked around the room hoping to spot an attendant, a care giver, a nurse, someone who would be willing to wheel Damien away but the only ones near us were the men, playing their table games or sitting idly, glazed to the TV set in the corner. I wanted to scream out, to yell for help. The idea of organizing what I had heard into a presentation for my fellow students and professors in the department seemed to lose its importance. Fear paralyzed me, making it impossible to move or to run.

More intent on telling his story then being a witness to my reactions, he continued. "So, Eli waited... waited until Margaret had turned her back, and he plunged the metal rod," imitating the force with his arm raised, "right into the back of her skull."

I looked in horror at Damien's wheelchair and realized how one of these long, metal spokes if used as a weapon and applied with enough force could easily be shoved right through one's skull. The newspaper account never actually detailed how Margaret Sullivan had met her demise, other than to say that she had been stabbed to death. The whole idea of dressing up in another patient's clothing, feigning identity, and waiting like an animal ready to feast on its prey made me shiver. According to what I had read, Damien had actually thought he would get away with his crime complete to pinning the act on someone else. I had the real story now, told from Damien's perspective, and that is what I had come to Eloise for.

Casually, I tried to thank the man for his time, for his information, hoping he wouldn't be able to see my legs, hidden in my black slacks, trembling, nor my hands shaking. One thing was clear to me. As paradoxical as it sounded, Damien was still less a threat here in the institution than he would be to walk the streets. Without a doubt, Damien belonged here in this crazy house, as he had put it.

***

A week later, I crossed myself three times in thanksgiving that I had finally completed the typed report that I planned to present tomorrow in Walter Hall. If successfully received, I would be exempt from taking my finals and would welcome starting my fourth year of studies at Argonaut University. I sat at my computer and rubbed my hands over my forehead. In the distance, I could hear the bellowing of thunder, and from the recent radio report, it was evident the effects of Hurricane Henry, hundreds of miles to the west, were heading my way. The roaring claps, much like the howling of caged lions in a zoo exhibit, repeated incessantly. I ran my hand over the back of my neck and got up to stretch my tired shoulders. I bent over and gathered the one-hundred sheets of my presentation and began to stack them into a pile.

"Tanya"

I turned my head and looked over my shoulder.

"Do you really think you're any different than Damien?"

***

A month after the holidays and still no one had taken the time to remove the twelve-foot Christmas tree, covered in clusters of plastic-colored balls and red-and-green twinkling lights, which stood in the center of the parlor. Along the walls were strings of pine garland, and from the windows hung small stockings, one for each patient on Ward D. Puffs of snow fell from the darkened clouds and landed on the pedestrians passing by the Eloise Mental Hospital, all in too much of a rush to stop, to care, for those committed inside its walls.

Damien blinked hard, and as he was about to reminisce about his past Christmases as a boy, he turned to the voice of a care giver.

"Damien, I'd like for you to meet a newcomer to Ward D, patient #0494773. Her name is Tanya."

Damien reached out his hand. "Haven't we met before?" he asked.

OF SHADOW & SUBSTANCE

Suzie Lockhart and Bruce Lockhart 2nd

Wyatt Drake leaned against the wall of the recreation room, taking long, slow drags from his Marlboro. He blew little smoke rings towards the browning wallpaper, trying to copy the size of the circles dotting the hideous pattern.

God, how he detested working at Shade River State Asylum. He hated all the crazies in it.

Wyatt couldn't image spending his life inside such a wretched place; he despised it beyond words. He could hardly wait until his shift was over so he could go home and sleep for a few hours. When he woke, he knew his mother would have a hot breakfast waiting for him.

"*Creak, creak, creak.*"

He'd been trying to tune out the annoying sound of Lyle, rocking back and forth in his chair as he muttered to himself. It wasn't a rocking chair, so the wooden legs protested against the linoleum floor with each movement.

It was enough to drive any sane person crazy.

The loathing inside of him bubbled to the surface, and he crushed his cigarette butt against the wall before tossing the remains into an ashtray.

Lyle was a schizophrenic who was obsessed with comic books, especially the Batman series. He fancied himself some sort of super villain; one that the dark knight was always chasing. Humph. Some super villain.

He was pathetic.

Wyatt doubted Lyle could hurt a fly.

But Wyatt could hurt *him*…

He slid noiselessly across the room until he was standing behind the disturbed patient. "Bats is coming for you," he hissed in Lyle's ear.

Lyle's reaction was instantaneous. He began screeching in terror as he hopped out of the chair, toppling it over. His hands began flapping as he screamed in distress.

"Augh! AUGH!" He ran around the room screaming and cursing and then he fell on the floor. He scooted into a corner of the room, sitting with his knees pulled up to his chest as he tried to hide from the imaginary threat. Just the reaction Wyatt had been hoping for. A sneer curled the corners of Wyatt's lips.

Wyatt was the real threat, not Batman.

He walked over and yanked the thinner man to his feet, roughly pulling his arms behind his back.

"Lyle, I think you need to cool off." He began dragging Lyle through the door.

Now he could blow off some steam.

"Augh! No! Nooo…!"

Wyatt just laughed coldly. He would have his fun before Cheryl came on duty at eight. Unfortunately, she didn't appreciate his sense of humor.

He didn't wanna piss Cheryl off.

What Wyatt wanted to do, was ask her out.

She was hot, in a high society kinda way. Sort of like Kennedy's wife.

Not that Wyatt much cared for Kennedy.

But he would do the President's wife.

In a minute.

Lyle was weak from his years spent at Shade River State Asylum and Wyatt pulled him effortlessly down the hallway. His cold laugh echoed through the sickly yellow walls; the fluorescent light illuminating the peeling paint.

Lyle stopped struggling about halfway down the hallway. He knew what was coming and knew there was nothing he could do to stop it.

One of his partners in crime met him at the end and together they stripped Lyle's clothes off and tossed him in the shower room. Wyatt turned the cold water from the hose on full blast, and the two orderlies hooted with brutal laughter as Lyle curled into a ball, huddling in the corner. He was so thin that his spine was visible under his waxen skin.

After fifteen minutes or so of the torment, Wyatt got bored. He shut the hose off and offered up a threat to the shivering, naked man.

"Now, you behave or I'll have to bring you back here." He tossed his clothes into a puddle on the floor and commanded, "Get dressed."

After securing Lyle in his room, he headed back to the recreation room. A black man diagnosed with multiple personality disorder, who he enjoyed messing with was there, along with a meek woman named Iris that he'd heard had been abused in 'unspeakable' ways by her own mother.

Wyatt referred to the black man as Mr. Ed, 'cause he thought he looked like a horse from the TV show.

The clock on the wall stated that it was almost eight. Cheryl would arrive soon for her shift. As he sucked on his cigarette, he contemplated what other horrors he could inflict on his wards before she arrived to quell the monotony.

He made a mental note to deal with Iris later. Wyatt's eyes traveled to the small television set sitting in the corner. He knew exactly what would freak her out.

And he could agitate Iris without Cheryl realizing what he'd done.

Wyatt wasn't even sure what he had against Iris, other than her weird problem with his favorite TV show.

Man, it was a great show. He'd loved an episode a few weeks back, when a kid who was a little menace kept sending people to the cornfield. Wyatt kept trying to decide if he'd want to hang with the kid or kill him.

Ever since he'd first seen the episode about the guy who just wanted to read and then was left all alone with all the books he wanted, but had no glasses, he was hooked. It made him chuckle just thinking about how twisted it was.

Aw, damn, he'd missed his opportunity. Cheryl would be in any minute. Fun would be put on hold. He fished out another Marlboro.

"Hey, Wy," Cheryl greeted him as she sauntered into the room. "Can I get one of those?"

He grinned at the pretty nurse as he handed her one, letting his hand linger on her soft skin for a moment. It was incredible that the attractive brunette could make even one of those dark dresses with the hideous white apron, look good.

"Anything you want baby." He offered suggestively.

She smiled back. As she stuck the cigarette between a pair of brightly colored lips, he began to get aroused. He held the lighter up and she bent nearer as he flicked it on. Cheryl must've just had her hair done. Wyatt caught the fresh hairspray scent as he sniffed at her coiffed locks, partially covered by her nurses' hat.

He wished he could get her alone sometime. He'd show her what it was like to be with a *real* man, instead of that loser boyfriend she was always talking about.

Distracted by the sound of a car, he saw that several patients were huddled around the TV watching Route 66.

"Man, that's a sweet ride."

"Mmm," Cheryl agreed.

"I think you're looking at Buz, not the Corvette," Wyatt scowled.

Cheryl flipped her head back and laughed. "I gotta get back to work."

This pissed Wyatt off and he decided he didn't feel like watching the show anymore. He stomped over and changed the channel.

"Hey!" A few of the patients protested while Wyatt glared at them, challenging any one of them to defy him.

"Shut up!" he demanded. He left a stupid war show on, flattened the cigarette butt in the ashtray and stormed out of the room. He felt like sending everyone to the cornfield right then.

If only he could get Cheryl alone.

"Break time," he called out as he passed the nurses' station. He shoved open the heavy metal door under the exit sign and took two steps at a time, until he reached the bottom.

A blast of bitter air hit him in the face as he stepped outside, sending him into a coughing fit. He rushed across the parking lot and opened the door of his rundown Ford. He slid inside and lit up another smoke, stretching his long legs out diagonally in front of him as he leaned back in the seat and propped his feet up on the dash. He started up the engine and cranked on the heat, as he stared blankly at the looming structure in front of him. The moonlight was casting an eerie glow on one of the corner towers.

Wyatt would hate to be a patient in one of these loony bins.

Especially this one.

He tossed his cigarette out the window, watching the ashes flicker to the ground and sizzle out as they hit the damp asphalt.

He clicked on the radio, listening to Connie Francis' mournful voice fill the car. He grabbed a sandwich out of a brown paper bag that his mother had packed for him. After wolfing it down, he grabbed the frosty bottle of grape soda lying on the back seat. The chilled Nehi tickled his throat, making him cough. A few purplish spots splattered the white uniform. He grabbed a tissue and tried to blot it.

"Damn."

Wyatt sighed heavily. Time to go back to the hell hole.

After shutting off the radio and cutting the engine, Wyatt pocketed his car keys and dragged himself towards the North tower. He was overcome with a discomfiting sensation of déjà vu as he reached the doorway. Shrugging it off, he headed inside.

By the time he reached the third floor, it was pushing nine-thirty.

Cheryl was nowhere to be found, so he walked over to Mr. Ed. Taking on an official sounding tone, he told him, "Sir, the Russians are threatening to fire their nukes."

The middle-aged man rose from his seat. "Thank you, Mr. Vice-President."

Edward Johnson began pacing back and forth across the black and white tiles, holding his hand near his head as he spoke into a phantom phone. He even held his other hand as if it were wrapped around a cord. Wyatt chuckled to himself, amused at the notion of a black man believing he was the President.

Iris was sitting quietly in the corner, absorbed in her knitting. She didn't notice the channel had been changed until the hair-raising music began and Rod Sterling's riveting voice began the opening dialogue.

"You unlock this door with the key of imagination. Beyond it is another dimension – a dimension of sound, a dimension of sight, a dimension of mind. You're moving into a land of both shadow and substance, of things and ideas. You've just crossed over into the Twilight Zone."

Sterling had barely started his mantra before Iris began flipping out, crying and moaning in her seat as she raked her hands down her face. With each word the television spoke, her agitation grew, until it reached a boiling point.

Iris flew out of her seat, accidentally bumping into a large framed woman, who always dressed like a guy. She went to punch Iris, who ducked, and the blow landed on someone else. The whole place erupted into chaos! Before more orderlies could reach the room, a heavy lamp landed on the side of Wyatt's head.

Mr. Ed stood over Wyatt's limp form, the brass lamp still clutched in his grasp. Shaking his head, he stated gravely, "Russian bastards."

***

"Wh… what happened?"

"You're okay, Mr. Drake. You just had another episode." A young black girl was peering through the dimness at him wearing something that looked like the orderlies' uniforms, except even in the low lighting he could see the color was bright turquoise.

"Get the hell away from me, girl!" he ordered, then was caught up in a fit of coughs.

The girl sighed. "Mr. Drake, you need to take it easy, *sir*. You're gonna make yourself sick again."

"What the hell? Where am I?"

"You're at Shade River State Asylum, in Reedsville, Ohio. Remember?"

Wyatt tried to stand in order to get away from this crazy black girl, who he was certain must be a new patient or something.

He found, however, that he couldn't move the bottom half of his body. When he looked down, Wyatt discovered that he was sitting in a wheelchair, with a black and red plaid blanket folded on his lap. The hands resting on the blanket belonged to some old guy. They were pale and thin and wrinkled, and had brown splotches all over them.

When Wyatt moved his hands, the old guy's hands moved.

His mouth fell open. Was this some twisted, sick joke?

"Help!" he shouted. "Help me! Help!"

"Mr. Drake, you really must calm down…" Wyatt's frail body shook with a series of painful coughs. "Damn!" The girl in the turquoise scrubs cursed and ran to the door.

The coughing fit continued. Wyatt struggled to breathe. He felt as if he might throw up.

"Ed, he's havin' another episode. Help me get him in bed."

Wyatt's eyes widened in horror as a black man in his mid-forties headed towards him; he instantly recognized him as Mr. Ed.

"Don't… touch… me," he spat between coughing fits.

Both ignored his protests as they lifted him up and laid him flat on the bed. Ed grabbed an oxygen mask and placed it over Wyatt's mouth and nose.

"Breathe, Mr. Drake. You gotta calm down."

With that, he passed out.

***

"Wyatt, Wyatt, are you okay?" A voice that must belong to an angel reached his ears. No, wait, it was Cheryl! Wyatt forced his eyes open to find Cheryl hovering over him. He forced himself to sit up, gasping for breath as his chest heaved heavily.

A bad dream. That's all it had been.

"I'm worried you might have a concussion."

Seeing the deep concern in her gray eyes made everything better. Wyatt liked the way she used heavy black liner on her lids, drawing them to the corners in such a way that she looked like some Egyptian queen.

It was a real turn-on.

He rubbed his left temple; it was throbbing viciously.

"Maybe you should see a doctor, Wy." Her hand was on his thigh. No doctor. He didn't want her to see any weakness.

With great effort, he pulled himself to his feet. He kept his hand on the back of a chair, waiting for the room to stop spinning.

"I'm fine, honey, really. I just need a cigarette. Besides, my shift is over. I'll just go home and sleep it off."

He cautiously made his way around to the front of the chair and lowered his large frame into it. He saw that the recreation room had been cleared. Good, because he was really pissed off at whoever did this to him.

When he found out just who it was, he would make them pay.

Wyatt pulled out two Marlboros and handed one to Cheryl. She took the seat next to him.

"I really wish you would let one of the doctors take a look at you."

He shook his head. "Not much they can do for a concussion. I'll be fine. I'm off tomorrow. I'll rest up, okay?"

Wyatt was thoroughly enjoying all the concern and attention she was lavishing on him. He wondered if this would be a good time to ask her out. It might make it look like he was trying to take advantage of the situation.

Which he would be.

So instead of asking her out, he told her, "You can even call and check on me if you want."

"I might just do that," Cheryl said.

An hour later, Wyatt carefully headed for home. A surreal sensation surrounded him as he carefully made his way through the back roads that lead to his modest home. The trees seemed to bend towards the road; their bare branches like menacing fingers as they swiped at his car. Shivering, he shifted gears and sped up, even though he was still feeling more than a little off-kilter.

Relief washed over him as his house came into view. He pulled into the driveway and hurried up the stone steps. Wyatt flung open the door.

His mother was asleep on the couch. Hearing the door, she stirred.

"Hi, honey," she mumbled. Then she saw the bump on his head and tossed off the bedspread that covered her. "Oh my God, Wyatt! What happened?"

She rushed over and began fussing over him, like mothers do. Wyatt's father had died several years ago, so Wyatt was all she had.

After reassuring her that he was okay, he headed towards his room. He felt a little nauseated, so he sat down on his twin bed and lit up a cigarette. After a few puffs, he only felt worse. He extinguished it carefully, saving the rest for morning.

A good night's sleep was all he needed, he told himself.

Yet, there was a part of him that was afraid to go to sleep.

When he was out before, that bad dream seemed so real…

"You're being a pussy," he told himself. He stripped down to his boxers and slid under the cool sheets. A sense of euphoria and ease washed over him as he shut his eyes.

But as familiar music played in his head, his relief was short lived…

***

When Wyatt awoke several hours later, a white woman that he recognized who must be a nurse, even though she wasn't dressed like any nurse he'd ever seen, was fiddling with IV bags hanging over his head.

"Mr. Drake, you're awake. Good. How are you feeling?"

All he could do was stare at Iris's made-up face. With her hair streaked blonde and make-up on, she was actually sort of attractive.

Wyatt was so freaked out that he couldn't answer. He kept blinking his eyes, hoping that when he opened them back up, this nightmare would dissolve into thin air and he'd wake up, back in his bed. As a nasty odor assaulted his nostrils, he wrinkled his nose in disgust.

"I'm going to get an aide so we can get you cleaned up."

To his mortification, Wyatt realized the smell was coming from him. This was all too much. Tears leaked out of the corners of his eyes.

Iris came back with Ed and they cleaned him up. It was the most humiliating experience he had ever endured in his life.

His life! How could he instantly go from being twenty-six to being an old man?

"What day is it?" He croaked.

"It's Friday, old timer." Ed told him.

"No, I mean the date. What is the date?"

"October 12."

"And... the year?"

Wyatt waited with baited breath for the answer.

"2012."

A loud gasp escaped his lips. Why that meant he was… seventy-six?! This had to be another crazy-ass dream. His mind was playing tricks on him; feeding off of the other dream. That was all. He'd wake back up, in his bed… soon.

A fleeting thought ran through his head. Maybe he should be nicer toward the loons at the Asylum.

"No!" He protested. "No! It's 1962!"

Edward Johnson shook his head sadly.

"Prove it!" Wyatt demanded, his voice strained. "Bring me a newspaper."

Sighing, Ed said, "I'll see what I can do."

"And cigarettes," he shouted after him, before several coughs escaped his ravaged lungs.

Wyatt's eyes traveled to the television set across from his bed. It was unlike anything he'd ever seen. The screen was flat and there was no box behind it. How did they do that?

The news was on and they were talking about the President. To Wyatt's astonishment, a black man popped up on the screen. He was tall and distinguished looking, and was speaking to a crowd of supporters in a very distinct voice. Again, all Wyatt could do was stare. He couldn't believe it.

Wyatt wished he could get up and change the channel, but even if he could get up, there were no visible knobs on that contraption.

This wasn't just a bad dream.

It was a fuckin' nightmare.

***

Wyatt was startled awake by a scraping noise.

When he opened his eyes, he found himself sitting in a chair in the recreation room at Shade River.

Lyle was next to him, rocking back and forth. He was grinning at Wyatt like an idiot.

"What are you looking at," he questioned.

"You were asleep. Better watch out, Batman might get you."

Lyle began laughing uncontrollably.

Wyatt stood and rushed out of the room. He half-ran to the nurses' station.

His knuckles were white as he grasped the counter. Breathlessly, he asked, "What day is it?"

"Why, Wyatt, it's Monday. What's wrong? Are you okay?"

He shook his head. "I'm not sure."

Cheryl led him to a seat behind the counter and made him sit down. She felt his head.

"I told you to see the doctor, Wy. Concussions can be serious business."

Wyatt's voice was shaky as he whispered to Cheryl, "I don't remember driving here. I don't remember anything between now and Friday night, when I went to bed."

A small gasp escaped Cheryl's painted lips. She grabbed his arm. "C'mon, you need to take it easy."

She led him to an empty room, urging him to lie down and rest. "The doctor will be making rounds shortly. I'm going to ask him to look in on you, Okay?"

Wyatt nodded his head in reluctant agreement because he was terrified.

***

Wyatt didn't remember dosing off, but when he woke, he was old again.

Useless...

A nurse with dark hair poked her head inside the doorway. "Mr. Drake, your doctor is here to take a quick peek at you."

"Cheryl," he croaked. "Oh, Cheryl, tell me what's going on." Tears were flowing again. "Can you get me a cigarette?"

"Now, Mr. Drake, you know you're not supposed to smoke anymore. They already had to remove one lung."

Wyatt's hand automatically flew to his chest and, sure enough, he felt a fine scar on the right side.

"Cheryl...?"

He could see the pity in her eyes, and it made him feel small.

And old.

She patted his hand, offering kind words.

Wyatt was only halfway surprised when Lyle came walking into the room, in this twisted future place. He was wearing pleated trousers and an expensive looking tie. He also wore a white doctor's coat.

"Mr. Drake, I'm going to add a medication called Aricept. It will help you with your cognitive function. It may help with some of your… memory issues." He scribbled something on a small pad and tore off a sheet, then handed it to Cheryl. "I hear you've had a rough couple of days." He patted Wyatt's shoulder.

Wyatt spat at him.

Doctor Lyle glared at him, then went to the sink to wash up.

Cheryl was standing over him with a disappointed look creasing her brow. "That wasn't very nice." She chastised.

Wyatt shut his eyes tightly and tried to will himself back to his life.

***

Later that night, Wyatt found himself sitting in front of the flat screen TV in the recreation room. He was gazing at a Batman movie, in disbelief at how true-to-life it was. He was mesmerized and a little fearful.

And a little fearful. These newfangled TVs made everything look so authentic.

He couldn't imagine how they made Gotham City look so real. So real, that you felt you could walk right into it.

Wyatt sighed. He wondered if he would have a chance to go back again. Remorse was beginning to eat away at him. He had done some vile deeds. He would maybe say that he was sorry.

Maybe.

He would ask Cheryl out.

He would tell his mother he loved her. Wyatt hadn't said those words to her since he was a kid. And she took care of him. Since his father passed away, Wyatt became her life.

He hadn't really appreciated all she did.

Regret overwhelmed him.

What if he never went back?

He must have dozed off, because all of a sudden, familiar music began to play; rousing him awake.

"You unlock this door with the key of imagination." The voice beckoned to him.

"Beyond it is another dimension - a dimension of sound, a dimension of sight, a dimension of mind. You're moving into a land of both shadow and substance, of things and ideas."

His eyes widened as a shadowy figure seemed to move towards him, leaning out of the TV. He seemed to be speaking directly to him as he said, *"Mr. Wyatt Drake, you've just crossed over into the Twilight Zone."*

WINDOWS TO THE SOUL

A.A. Garrison

Why'd I kill them folk? Well, that there's a big hairy question, son, and I just might answer it. But let's first get something straight. You ain't here for *why* nothing. You come to hear old Barnaby Rick say a bunch of crazy shit for your paper. And that's okay, we all gotta eat. I'm gonna have to disappoint, though, because this boy ain't crazy, straitjacket or not.

Okay. Yeah. Why the killing.

My first was this whore in the town I's born, on account of her hurting me in a bad way. A hateful bitch, of the likes they warned you of in the Bible. I saw it in her eyes, right off the bat. Made me sick. I tried and help her, and she hurt me for it, so I killed her. Simple. Probably better off, but that's neither here nor there.

How'd I know her trade? Told you, was in the eyes. Windows to the soul? For me, that's literal - or *was*, I guess. Heh. See, back then, I could look in a body's eyes and something would *click*, in my head like, and I'd *know* that person, could *be* them, about. Had it all my life, long's I can remember. Thought everyone was like that, until I's about sixteen or so. Now, it wasn't nothing psychic or supernatural or what have you - *uncommon*, maybe, but that's it. I couldn't see specifics, like what you had for lunch, but I could sure tell if it was sitting wrong with you. I'm just sensitive, is all. I just see what is, I suppose.

And I don't need to see your eyes to know what *you're* thinking, that old Barnaby Rick's crazy as they come. Don't be afraid and say it, son, you ain't alone. I don't spite you, just like I don't spite these head-shrink fellers in here. They got all kinds of lingo for my sensitivity: *delusional* and *schizoid*, and big-ass words I can't even say - probably even got some made special, just for me. But that's okay. It's their way. Got to label everything, so's they can belittle it and cram it in a box and shelf it away. And that goes double for folk like me, those that leave them scratching they heads. Got to make sure there's some five-dollar 'disorder' to slap me with. Funny who says what's right and proper, and what ain't. If the world shit in diapers, they'd have *continence* a disorder. Outlaw the commodes!

But yeah, that whore, she had it coming. That make it right? Hell no, and I'll be the first to tell you. I'll bet you think you know how it went down - business transaction, right? Wrong.

Listen up, son.

She was hitching, is how it come to pass, hitching down a lonely road in the middle of the night - - a *cold* night. Can get right cold in them mountains, colder than you know. I's in my truck and heading home from work when I seen her along the curb, with ass-hugging jeans and a halter top and tits here to Tuesday - suicide blonde too, gave definition to it. At first I just went on - don't borrow trouble, yeah? But then my conscience got hold of me, so I doubled back and picked her up - and that's when I got a look in them eyes. They plumb whacked me in the face, right there alongside the road - because that's how it happens, that click I told you about. Them eyes said she was a user, a people-user - someone who'd been used and let it *sour* her - let it become her, so's she passed it on to others. Share the love. Wasn't whoring for the money, no was so she could spray that hurt around, maybe with some critters and a disease in the bargain. It was... *vampiric*, that's the word. Except, she was a vampire you bit first.

That wasn't why I killed her, though. That just made me sick and I's used to being sick a long time before then, just from getting clicked every time I made a body's eyes. Ha! No, was what come later that brought out my killing man.

So, Miss Used-So-Now-I-Use is in my truck, getting to know the heater. I ask where she's going. She sits there shivering, and looking me up and down with them speaking eyes and gives me a street. We made some small talk on the way, the woman clicking me the whole time. The street was dead empty, just this little mud road way out in a holler, nothing but us and the pines - probably where she took her tricks, truth be known. I get her there and stop - but she don't leave, just sets there eyeballing me in a way I don't like. "I'd liked to thank ye for the ride," she says, coming closer and closer, enough so's I could smell trashy perfume. I told her no, right then, wasn't in the market, but she just giggled and says this ain't no sale. I crush up against my door and she just comes closer, with that dopey face that says oversexed and under-smart. Then she threw a hand on my jewels - and that cost her life.

She puts out her hand and gives me a good, learned squeeze, and her face changed. "You *want* it," she says. "You're harder than cold granite." And that pushed a button in my head - because yeah, maybe a part of me *did* want it, that cold lizard in every man, who don't know Jezebel from the love of your life. That's what hurt me the most, I think, seeing that in me - that any of me would want her. It left me sicker than ever - *smothered* in sick, her sick, like she'd throwed a bucket. I just wanted her gone, but she kept calling me names and honking her titties and getting all loud and rowdy. *Harridan* is the word. Or, bitch. She was a textbook bitch, bitchery all around.

I don't remember deciding to do it. I think I blacked out for a spell, because out of nowhere her throat's in my hands and I'm squeezing, and she's wearing a new, panicked face - but innocent too... how she might of looked when step-daddy took her in the tool shed. I knew it was wrong, even as I's doing it, especially after seeing that little girl in there. And besides, I *should've* been the bigger man - fight with monsters and you become one, or however it goes. But I didn't stop choking. I *was* crazy then. Was kind of outside myself, don't know the word. You'll have to ask the shrinks in here.

Did I break down when I realized what I done? No, not hardly: I *liked* the killing. I won't deny it. It got me harder than I already was or ever been - my heart all juiced and hammering, head jacked like I been into some dope. There was an intimacy there too, maybe the only real kind. So yeah, it was wrong, sure, but I liked it and anyone who's took a life and said otherwise is a liar. There's a freedom in it, see, you just letting go and doing what comes natural.

But don't get me wrong: killing's a trap. *Deceptive*, like. See, that freedom's just an *illusion*, from you giving in to your animal self - to your hate and anger, and that killing man what lives in everybody. And there ain't no pain there neither, is a way to run from pain, hide from it in that killing man's shadow. But, understand: that ain't freedom, but just a lack of restraint. Folk think it's strong killing somebody, but that's a god-honest lie. Strength is facing your pain and fear instead of running from it - *resolving* it. No, killing's for the *weak*... folk too lost in themselves to know they're so. You wanna be strong, forgive the son of a bitch and be done with it.

Anyhow. That was my first, the whore. Never did catch a name. Once I got use of my body again, I drug her into them woods and throwed her in a glen and run off

They never did find her or nothing. Nobody would ever have known, if I ain't confessed.

And I know what you're thinking now, son: Okay, maybe his head-clicking ain't crazy and maybe he wasn't crazy for killing the bitch, but he's *sure* crazy for killing them other two and for what he done to himself. Right? Well, I'm telling you: I ain't crazy.

The second was at the grocery I worked for years.

I was a cashier up front and that was hell, I tell you. All day seeing that drugged look folk get at the waterhole, me clicking like the gol-darn Wheel of Fortune. You'd think I'd pick some other job, with my condition, but them was hard times and it was the grocery or starve. Sometimes you just got to do what you got to do. It could've been worse, I guess. Could've ended up an eye doctor.

It happened in a holdup, the killing. Now, I'd been held up twice before all this mess and it really didn't bother me none, just give up the green like I been told and the crook be on his way. It scared me more getting clicked than seeing a gun. But this holdup was different. This feller was *evil*.

Though, I don't know if that's the word. If there's one thing I've learned in this life of mine, it's that evil's funny. It ain't that it don't exist *period*, like some folk say these days, it's just subjective, not easy to judge - something seen through a glass darkly, if you dig. I know that just from seeing behind folks' eyes all them years, knowing what makes people tick - or what makes them tock, at least. I've given the subject a lot of thought, since I ain't evil. I just got riled and lost my head and done wrong, and I think that's typical of what most would call evil, more or less. The way I see it, we're all good and bad both... just depends on the time of day and who you ask.

But not when it came to that robber I killed. He was purest evil because he knew what he was doing, knew it and liked it.

He come in through the line like everyone else, no mask or nothing. I caught his eyes and I saw something wrong - but then, about *everybody* has something wrong, see. If I made a fuss whenever I see the devil in a body's eyes, wouldn't get no folk checked out. This boy, his eyes were all starey and bloodshot, and I thought dope, though anyone in a market looks doped. But I didn't think much of him, until it's his turn and up comes a gun. I looked in his face then - a good hard look, him looking *back* this time, which makes a difference - I looked in his face and he clicked me and that's when I saw the evil.

I got this sprung joy from him, see, like a kid in a circus. In fact, when I was in his head, that's just what I saw, a punk little boy making someone small and scared and loving it. Now, *I* wasn't scared, bullets and hurt don't scare me - I have that *other* fear - of that *head*-hurt, which I've taken care of since. But the people in line, the animals at the waterhole? *They* were scared, yes sir, and that boy, the lion, he was drinking it in. Really, you didn't need no click to read that boy: a truck could've passed through his smile.

So, up comes the gun and I started feeling sick right then, how I do when I click anyone who don't rub me right. I told myself no, I'd just hand over the money and let him go - but I *couldn't* just let him go, because this punk wouldn't stop here or with the next heist or the next. That boy got off on it, would probably go on doing stick-'em-ups with a million in the bank. And *that* was what got me - that and the joy and an ugly eagerness too, him just waiting for me to get brave so he could start shooting. His sick filled me up, all but making my eyes float.

I knew then someone was going to die - him or me.

I saw it coming... could feel my killing man waking up and reaching for the wheel, but I was helpless to interfere. It was just like the first time, me outside my own head, watching it happen with the rest of the store. I saw myself take out a fistful of bills and start shoving them into the bag - then I uppercut the gun away and shot across the checkout, his neck in my hands and going white. He fought a fair bit, fetched me a couple good ones over the head, but I didn't feel nothing - the killer took them blows, not me.

As it turned out, though, I had mercy on that boy. Or tried to, at least.

What happened was, he stopped fighting and fell back, and I saw another side of him - just like the whore. He changed to that kid I'd seen earlier, the little bastard who'd gotten himself a big old body and a big old dick and a big old ego but was still just a little bastard. Evil or not, that boy deserved a chance and before I know it, I'm letting off and staggering away. But the boy didn't move. Me and some other folk tried and perk him up, breathing into him and pumping his chest and whatnot, but he kept dead, still with that boyish look to him even when the meat men hauled him off.

I was broken up after that one, because of jail mostly. But lucky for me, this was nineteen and seventy-nine in the deep south and there wasn't no one bleeding-heart enough to try me for making some boy dead when he had a gun in my face. It was swept under the rug, nobody saying nothing and memories getting short. Even had some folk calling me a hero. Hoo-wee! Barnaby Rick, a hero. And they say I'm crazy.

There were hard days then. I got bad scared after I sent that boy to earth. Couldn't make nobody's eyes, for fear of finding bad there and catching it. Nightmares every night, blood on my hands. I'm surprised I didn't fix things then and there. Still, I ended up quitting the grocery for a career in the bottle. I drank up everything I had and then went on the street for a good while - which was better than the straight world, I got to say. Yellow as it was, the boozing really did set me right - can't make a body's eyes when you can't see straight. Of course, the booze brought its own problems, which would lead to the real fix. But that comes later.

I don't know how long I was on the street. At least that winter - I remember some of them cold mountain nights I told you about - but not no more than a year, because by eighty-one I was with my best friend, this Mehicano boy named Rick. Me and Rick went way back, grew up together, went hell-raising when we were younger. Rick and Rick they called us. So, Rick takes me in, straight-up charity. It was him and me and his girl Willy cramped up in this chintzy shoebox apartment out where nobody's proud of their address. He said he would've done it sooner, but he was down in Mehico, running dope.

I loved Rick like a brother and only more after we bunked up. Still can't believe I killed him.

Women are strange, the strangest of God's creatures. The pretty ones can be ugly - like that one I killed - and the not-so-pretties, beautiful. Like Willy, Rick's girl. It wasn't that she was *ugly* ugly, but just plain. I can still see her in my head, where the outside world used to be: frizzy brown hair, skinny, no titties to speak of. But woo! that girl had something. I don't know if there's a name for it but it drove me nuts. It was in her eyes, like everything that's real in this world. Rick, I'm sure he caught it too, just probably didn't know it. Everybody knows a good thing when they see it even if they don't.

Now, nothing would've come of it if she ain't been sweet on me in return. Everything could've been different - Rick still alive, me out of here and unfixed, Willy too. But I knew she was into me from the first, in the same way I got things from anybody. I tried and ignore it, told myself she was just like that to all the boys, but she wasn't. No sir.

I mentioned old Rick was a dope-runner, hauling grass and black-tar up from the homeland. Well, he wasn't no kingpin or nothing, or even a real criminal, would just make a call and get a job when the well run dry. He'd hitchhike down, then buy a junk car and do his thing. Easy money and there was no catching Rick. Thing is, it took him away from the homestead a week at a stretch, leaving me and Willy alone.

I'd been off the streets for a few months when he first went south, and things were actually looking up some. Willy'd shown me how to get on the dole, in regards to my 'psychiatric problems' - which were just me too freaked out to face the world sober, mind you - but she got me on the dole and I was helping with the rent and food and all. The rest of my check went right back to Uncle Sam, by way of the local liquor store. Still, once Willy and me were alone for the first time, I was sober enough to see what she had in mind. Her eyes shone with it, clicking me good. We were eating in the kitchen at the time, Rick gone not an hour, and she looks at me and I look at her and we forget lunch and pounce, humping right there beside the sandwich fixings.

That week passed like a dream.

It was crazy, yeah, doing it right under Rick's nose and in his own place. We talked about stopping, and tried to, but once old Rick was out the house we were magnetized, and it never got no better. But that's what love does to you, I guess... brings that trance where everything will be alright forever. It's that energy what comes with it, the two of you like a completed circuit - brain chemistry, hormones and all. Or, maybe because it was so wrong; that has a way of spicing things up. Anyway, we got outright adventuresome, going at it when Rick was in the shower or at the Laundromat or sometimes just in the bathroom. I'd hate myself afterward, before and during too, and Willy was the same but good God, was just no help for it.

We got away with it for a year - or thought we did - and I know this'll damn me to hell, but it was the best time of my life. I stopped drinking, in time, because Willy, she made all that fear and shit get small. I even got so bold as to try the reefer that she and Rick doted on so much, though that didn't last - the stuff shot my sensitivity sky-high, the click turning into a bang, me looking in someone's eyes and forgetting who I was. Scary. Anyhow, the day it happened, Rick was going south and Willy and me was all but counting the seconds, her little nipples waving hi from behind her blouse, her eyes telling me all the nasty things she had lined up. So naturally, after Rick said his goodbyes, us two were overcome, clawing at each other like we was fighting, buttons shooting every which way. We never heard Rick come back inside.

We were doing it on the living room couch and when I saw Rick in the door, I thought it was just bad luck. But then I saw the revolver staring me down and I knew there wasn't no luck to it. Willy saw too and we stopped without getting up, with a big fat second where nobody said nothing. I made Rick's eyes then - all stretched and veiny and wild, they were - and I got me the worse click of my life: he'd known, maybe right from the start. The hurt I saw there, I can't even describe. It was one reason why, later, I did what I did, so I wouldn't have to see no hurt like it again.

"Rick," I said, all choked and funny, like when Willy'd do this thing with her mouth. It was all I could say, "Rick, Rick," him not saying nothing, just accusing me with them madman eyes. Willy started crying, God bless her, just bawling like a newborn and curling her skinny naked self into the couch. Rick ignored her, though. Rick was fixed purely on me.

"En mi *casa*," he goes, in his Tex-Mex Spanish - "In my house." Well, it was a welfare apartment, but I got his drift. He said it over and over, louder and louder, the gun gone to shaking. I knew there was trouble when old Rick started up in his native tongue. Rick was a good guy, but he had a crazy streak and that crazy Rick only knew Spanish.

If not for the drunks outside, it might've been *me* underground, instead of Rick.

Rick ain't bothered with the door, so when our drunk neighbors passed by we heard them good and loud. Rick swung around like they were the police - and it was my chance, and I didn't hesitate. It was like all the rest, me stepping out my head so's that killing man could steal in - except there wasn't supposed to be no killing, not that time. The last thing I wanted was Rick dead, and you got to know that, mister. It was an accident.

So, just like that, I jackrabbit forward and knock the gun skyward and start wrestling Rick. We danced all around, the gun waving about, Willy carrying on, and somehow we get out the door and in the hall. It was the third story, with a big yawning atrium going up and down and so we're doing the tango right at the stair head, me stark naked, Rick growling like a man possessed. Next thing I know, we're in one last tug-o-war for the gun and I'm winning it from him and he's jerking back - ass over teapot down the stairwell.

I'll never forget the look in his eyes. All at once, the crazy left them and there was just pure surprise, like he'd been sleepwalking and finally come to. He knew he was going to die, in that way we sometimes just know, and it all clicked into me and ain't yet left. I threw out and tried to catch him, but he took to them stairs like from a cannon - somersaulting and cartwheeling and barrel-rolling. Could hear bones snapping, these pulpy crunches like breaking boards. I thought he might stop at the landing but he just pinballed off the wall and went on, all the way down, hitting the floor with one last snap - a kind of *kerUNCH*, maybe the first bite of an apple - his neck, I'm pretty sure. Willy'd just come out, as luck would have it, and you ain't never heard such a scream.

Then comes another scream, from down below, an old lady - looking at *me*, the murderer, gun in hand, atop the stairs that the boy was just pushed down. Or so it looked to her.

Unfortunate for me, it would look the same to the cops.

It thawed Willy and me both and we shoot back inside and throw on some clothes and not a word between us, the gun going in the toilet reservoir because who knows how many bodies're on it. When I finally get downstairs to Rick, the old bag that found him goes tearing off and slams her door and locks it - not a good sign.

Rick was a sight. One arm was okay but the other was all kinked up, broken in so many places it wasn't but a squiggle over the floor. Both legs were cocked at screwball angles, like he's doing the Funky Chicken, his left foot high enough to scratch the small of his back. And his neck... it looked like he'd died trying to stand on his left ear, if that paints a picture.

Rick was as dead as a doornail. The police were there in minutes flat.

Long story short, Rick went to the morgue, yours truly went to jail, and Willy... oh, poor Willy. I met her once after the shit went down. I was in the county lockup - murder one and no bail - and she came to visit, all gussied up in heels and makeup and a dress. Pretty, maybe for the first time. Except for her eyes. They were ruined, weepy, red and thunderstruck, like she'd been run over by a bus. You could tell she was bad off and the click showed me just how much - and what was coming.

First I said to her was, "Don't do it, baby. I know it's bad, but don't, for me." But I knew it was hopeless. I told you, Willy was tough, but only so much. Things hurt her, got under her skin and stayed there as they do anybody strong enough to see things how they are. Hell, for all I know, she had the click too. She started bawling up the moment I saw her and all she could say was, "I'm sorry, Barney. Sorry, sorry." I pleaded with her not to do it, all but got on my knees and balled my hands, but she just kept on, with that dead look in her eyes - eyes of the damned, I guess. Somebody who's made their bed and has to lay in it.

I never found out how she did it. The obituary just said it was sudden.

And again, I know what you're thinking: Okay, so the click's just sensitivity, the whore just riled him up, the thug was just a thug, and Rick was just an accident. But if old Barnaby ain't crazy, why'd he *blind* himself?

Well, son, ain't that obvious?

I admit, I did go right crazy after Willy went seppuku. It was too much, being locked up on a crime I didn't do and jail miserable like hell and my woman leaving me all alone in the world. And the whole time, I'm still clicking to beat the band, seeing the ugly in everybody, the world feeling like nails in the skin. I puked up all I ate and picked fights that didn't need picking. No sleep, nightmares of Willy's and Rick's eyes the last I saw them, clicking me from the grave. But the worst eyes was in the mirror: a feller reaping what he'd sowed. Not even some good rye could've helped me then.

Nope, only one cure for that kind of sick.

Sure, it pretty much hung a crazy-sign around my neck, but I maintain my sanity. If *you* were holed up in that jail, seeing what I saw, you would've picked out your eyes with a bedspring too.

It was what sent me up to this here country club - which I can understand. Not too many sane folk have reason to turn out their lights. Even so, I still might've been able to live my darkness in the pen, but I ended up sealing my own fate. I was delirious after I done the deed, and not just from the pain and my circumstance and the morphine - more than anything, I was *relieved*. No more clicking! Ha! So when they asked why, I just told the truth, jabbering about being in other people's heads and the ghosts of them that I killed - and *I* wasn't crazy, not me, no sir. Apparently I mentioned the whore in the woods, and they found her, which didn't help none. So I can understand why I'd get stamped section-eight. I'd say I was crazy too, were I someone else - which I ain't never gonna be again, thanks to my little remedy. Heh.

No... clicking's all behind me now... and I'm better off.

So you go on, son. You write your column about crazy old Barnaby Rick and his tale of woe. I just ask one thing: give me a fair chance, eh? I've been carrying this cross since donkey's years, and I think folk should know that crazy is, ain't always as crazy does. You hear? Afte all, it could be *you* sitting blind in a straitjacket. You don't need no click to see in folks' heads. Just look inside your own.

GO FISH, GO

Sean Conway

The lawn sprinklers sounded like rattlesnakes. An unsettling, monotonous sound, coupled with Eddie Fish bouncing his knee rapid-fire, his rubber flip-flop tapping the stonework while he sucked cigarettes in long, desperate draws. I sat next to him, leaning forward in the thick heat to avoid pressing my sweaty back against the bench. I turned the plastic lighter over in my hand, looking down at it, calculating the hours I had left. I'd agreed, stupidly, to pull an overnight double, saying yes about ten minutes before the brown-out that quieted every single air conditioner on the unit. Out here, on this bench in the quad, it was ninety-four degrees. Upstairs, on the third floor, behind the locked doors and windows, could've been a hundred and ten easily.

Eddie took three or four hard pulls before exhaling in one long release that seemed to deflate him, smoke swirling from his mouth and nose, almost crawling from him like a ghost. I felt a track of sweat tickle down the side of my neck. I swatted at it like a fly.

"You almost done?"

Eddie stared straight ahead, like he had been for three consecutive cigarettes, maybe looking at the bed of dead roses against the flaking side of Ruth House, maybe seeing something else entirely, something not even here right now. He stopped motoring his knee, exhaled again, the cigarette down to a crinkled nub between his fingers.

"Eddie, whataya say, you done?"

Off to the right was the staff parking lot where ten or twelve cars were parked, including my Tacoma pick-up my brother had given me last winter. I didn't like to look at it while I was working, made me homesick. I'd take patients out for smokes and glance over at it despite my best intentions and imagine leaving, poking my elbow out the window and putting the end of the game on the radio. I loved driving late at night, the warm summer air, the desolation, the splash of moonlight strobing between the rooftops as I accelerated through the neighborhoods on my way out to Route 128.

"Okay John."

I turned back to Eddie. Still staring straight ahead, his eyes small and beady but wide too, unblinking and glazed and faraway. I guessed he was overmedicated today. But what did I know—I was just a babysitter really. The badge on my belt loop said Counselor, but I didn't do a hell of a lot of counseling. I handed out cigarettes mostly, took patients for walks or drove them to their various appointments with social workers or halfway house directors. Once or twice a shift I'd be part of a team of other counselors and nurses that tackled, wrestled, pinned and restrained men and women, with leather straps, to their metal beds.

My name is Juan Sebastian. Eddie calls me John—I don't know why. I stopped correcting him. I stood up and slipped the lighter into my back pocket, then waited for Eddie to get up. Still staring at the roses, his mouth twisted into a grin and he laughed quietly. Whatever it was in that head of his that entertained him like that, I wanted some of it. I hadn't laughed probably in close to a year.

***

Ruth House was up on the third floor, above the Admissions office and, on the second floor, the cafeteria. The giveaway that you're not just entering any old room is that the door to the unit is so heavy: a thick steel door that you really need a shoulder to get moving. There's a small glass pane in its center. We're trained to press our faces close to it as we're inserting the key, to take a peek into the unit before we enter, make sure there isn't a patient creeping around the corner waiting to catch the door and flee. A Flight Risk, is what we call it. Or *eloped,* after the fact. I looked left, right, a quick glance down best I could, then twisted the key and shouldered my way in, holding it for Eddie behind me, standing guard a moment while it banged closed hard enough to rattle the walls.

The density of heat was dizzying. Reminded me of the times I've had to venture up into the attic of my house in the height of July or August, the air dead and thick and my arms and neck almost instantly slick with sweat, which then reminded me to stop by the house one of these days and grab whatever I'd left up there, in the attic. It was the one part of the house I hadn't yet cleaned out. But Claudia was dating someone new now, according to my girls: a cop named Mateo, and so now I was probably going to need an appointment to visit what was supposed to be my own goddamn house.

Truth: appointment or no appointment, lately I'd been driving by after work, a little before midnight, just to see if there was any strange car there. So far there hadn't been, which is always a relief. But then I drive the rest of the way home feeling guilty and dirty for having crept by the house at ten miles an hour, looking at Claudia's Rav4 in the driveway, and at the single warm light in the kitchen window.

***

I felt a little like a hypocrite, writing down in the daily log what happened with my patients, their behaviors. I couldn't tell you why we do this; supposedly it's to debrief the next shift. But to me it always felt like it was just to go through the motions, pretend the job was something more than it really was. If there were any true incidents—violence, an eloper, some sort of inappropriate contact between patients—the head nurse on duty relayed that to the next shift during a quick meeting that preceded each shift. I never looked at the daily log for any other reason than to write my notes. I never read anyone else's. So they probably didn't read mine either.

E.F. presented as lethargic most of the p.m. Smoke break x 4. Attended morning meeting and A.T. [Activities Therapy], *met with social worker to discuss aftercare placement, but S.W. said patient didn't share much and appeared distracted, looking out the window, often disengaged.*

I'd learned the lingo of the reports, but the reality was I didn't really belong here. Nearly every other counselor was enrolled in a nursing program, or in grad school for social work, or a fresh-out-of-college Psych major. Everyone was, in one way or another, 'in the business.' I'd ended up here by a different route, one that couldn't help but make me feel a little lost and off-track, which, if I were being honest, I was. I'd landed the job because I was, first, a guy, and second, over two hundred pounds. They needed bodies as much as they needed wannabe social workers and psych nurses. No training, no background, but I was a presence, and every locked-door unit needed as many of those as it could get.

I hated the fact that Ruth House was as much a home to me as anywhere. Depressing but true. I'd only been in my small studio apartment a short while. Boxes still sa unpacked in every corner, since unpacking once and for al would make it permanent. Would make it *home.* I didn' want it to be. But the house wasn't home anymore either, that much was obvious. So this was it. Sixty hours most weeks. I gave in to doing doubles less for the money than the simple fact that I didn't want to walk into that empty apartment, to sit by myself with no cable and no food and the smell of cardboard everywhere. Sometimes I'd drive around for a couple hours, often longer, going nowhere. Maybe cruise by the old house, see what was what. Check for signs of Mateo. So I'd pull overnight doubles, catch a few Zs downstairs on the lobby sofa, and it was as good as anything right now.

"Am I gonna die, John?"

I walked around the tables of the common room, putting away board games. Parchesi, Sorry, Clue, Chutes & Ladders, Uncle Wiggly, Strawberry Shortcake. Old boxes broken at the edges, limp and musty, artifacts from a lifetime ago, all, missing cards, lacking pieces, some replaced with substitute pieces: bottle caps, erasers, pennies, and a toothpaste cap. I stacked them best they'd stack and then turned to poor old Eddie. He sat at a table, head in his hands like he was carrying an immeasurable burden. I guess he probably was. "Are you gonna die?" I asked.

His leg bounced, his white painter's pants too loose, fluttering like sails. The sleeves of his faded denim jacket were rolled, his stick-thin forearms and wrists crutching his head, pale and freckled. He never wore a shirt. Just the unbuttoned jacket, too short, too tight to properly close. I figured it must've been a freebie that had originally come from the Young Miss section of a department store. "No, you're not going to die," I told him. Then I shrugged. "Well, no time soon, anyway."

Shiever was nearby, looming with his arms behind his back, one hand holding the other wrist. Shiever was about fifty, bald, heavy, ghostly pale—like so many of them were—from a lack of natural light. He was legally blind. This conversation caught his interest and lured him over. I felt his stubby forefinger poke me. "Are you preserved?"

I sidestepped him so he couldn't do it again. His skin was clammy and slick. The blanket of heat was making me dizzy. "I'm not preserved, no. I'm still alive." He asked me this two or three times a day.

Eddie perked up. "What about me? Am I preserved?" His hair fanned up from his forehead, imprinted from his hands and stuck, like wire. I wondered when the last time he'd showered.

"Nope. Not preserved, Eddie. That's impossible." I kept thinking how much fun it would be to mess with these guys. Yeah, Eddie, you're fucking preserved. Whatever that even means. Yes, Shiever, you're pumped with preservatives too. Yes, David, the President of the United States is organizing a Special-Ops mission to break you out of here as we speak. Yes, Kenny, that's an eyeball growing at the base of your skull. As soon as it pops through the skin you'll be able to see in 360 degrees. But you couldn't do that. They'd taught me that first day: always redirect the patients back toward reality. Shoot straight with them. Not quite as fun, but whatever.

"I feel fucked up, John." Eddie's head was back in his hands. "I feel all fucked up."

Well, Eddie, that's because you *are* fucked up. You're frigging brain-damaged, dude. Your liver's dying, rotted by alcohol, and every synapse in your body has been burned dead with overmedication. I guess it's exactly how you *should* feel.

Instead: "You're all right, Eddie. You're all right." I picked up my clipboard to continue with my round of checks. "Maybe lie down or something. Go chill out." I walked away. It might have been the worst advice I'd ever given. Go lay down. The bed was where I did almost *all* my negative thinking. Thoughts and ideas and images strangling me. I tossed all night long, reliving the past, drawing up outrageous plans for the future that, by morning, revealed themselves under the clarity of sunlight to be the boneheaded ideas that they were. I hadn't slept more than three hours a night all summer. Sometimes I looked at the military-style beds, cots really, four to a room, and wondered if I belonged here myself. Without my keys, I mean.

***

Thea downstairs at the front desk called a Code Yellow for Grillo House just as I was taking a quick bite of a peanut butter and jelly English muffin sandwich; my third one this week. All these double shifts were keeping me away from the grocery store. Grillo House. There was always trouble over there. I covered a napkin over the top of the sandwich and wiped a hand on my pants. Grace poked her head in from the hall and told me to go. She was nurse manager and was here almost as much as I was. From what I knew, she was about forty-five, never colored her silver hair, and wore three or four of those rubber awareness bracelets, Lance Armstrong yellow ones but also blue and purple, and they dug into her pulpy wrists like tight flea collars. I think she told me once that she had a cat and two birds, but it might have been the other way around.

Ray was the other nurse on duty, rationing pills in the med closet, while Daphne and Rose leaned against the wall of the main hallway talking low to each other. They were the other two counselors working tonight, each about 99 pounds and not much use on a Code Yellow. "You got this one?" one of them asked. Somehow I still didn't know who was who.

"Back in a flash," I said, still trying to swipe peanut butter and bread from the pockets of my cheek and gum line with my tongue. I could see Eddie in the common area, sort of galloping the length of the long room, his jacket flapping open with each hop, a ropy arm swinging in a loose circle. For a second I thought he was having fun, some kind of sloppy version of the "Electric Slide." But I knew Eddie better than that. He didn't dance, that was for sure. His face was red and crumpled, grooved with trenches. I'd read once that he was 44 but he looked 60. *"I'm all fucked up!"* he kept saying over and over, electric sliding all the way down to the TV, then throwing his non-hips and coming back the other way, arm gunning and wild hair popping up and down. *"I'm all fucked up! I'm all fucked up! I'm all fucked up!"* The other three patients in the room, to their credit, or oblivion, watched TV with blank expressions.

I keyed the steel door open and said over my shoulder, "Eddie's all fucked up."

***

Halfway across the yard I heard Thea the front desk call, "Code Red, Grillo House. Code *Red*, Grillo House." I broke into a run. A Code Yellow was a synonym for "Show of Force," meaning someone was getting a little out of line, a little hard to handle, and the staff needed some backup, some support, just to show the patient that they meant business and these people were here to make sure the patient was complying. Usually that's all it took. Code Red was a different story: Code Red meant something had happened, something violent. A patient was hurting himself, or smashing something, or was fighting another patient. It meant for any and all available staff to get there immediately and get ready for something serious. Whatever the Code Yellow Show of Force had been about, it had just escalated into something probably a little scary.

It didn't take long to start sweating again, the air stiff and bogged down. In the distance I heard that monotonous tone that I always associated with hot summer days and swamps. Sounded like bugs but someone once said they were frogs, one long continuous tone, like a vibration.

A few other bodies charged out from the other units: Linkly House, where the adolescent unit was housed as well as some of the administration offices; Garret House, the substance abuse unit; and the Mackum Center, home of the A.T. department on the first floor, and the treatment center on the second floor. I caught, and passed, Jim Clovers pretty quickly. I'm not a small guy by any stretch, but Jim's pushing three hundred pounds, most of it hanging over his belt like a bean bag chair. "Race you," I said as I passed.

He was gulping air and couldn't seem to answer. Had it been a Code Yellow, I would have walked alongside him, but this wasn't a time for that kind of socializing. Grillo House could be a tough place sometimes. It was an admissions unit, for one, which meant every patient started on that unit, until they were properly diagnosed, set straight with their meds, had contracted for safety, and then, sometimes, moved along to other units better equipped to handle their individual issues.

I keyed into Grillo House without the usual cautious peek through the window, catching the door and considering holding it for Jim before realizing he was still several seconds behind me. I let it whip shut and moved down the narrow hall. This is what I never liked about Grillo House: it was old and small, tight corridors and lots of tiny rooms. Nooks everywhere. Just an old Colonial home remodeled as a locked-door shithouse. Ruth House was different: sitting above the hospital's main lobby, reception, and cafeteria, the unit was much more of an open concept, with a large common area in the middle and two large wings fanning out from either side, a men's wing and a women's wing. They coexisted in the common area, and one of our challenges was to keep them on their own sides, especially late at night.

But something here was wrong. I saw no one but heard something that reminded me of a jungle bird, a sound of low and long moans or cries, but quite loud. My first absurd thought was that there was an animal of some sort loose on the unit. Not seeing anyone was not a good sign. It meant staff had sent patients back to their rooms. I came by the small day room, also empty, and finally to the nurse's office, where three people, two I knew and one I didn't, were slapping rubber gloves over their wrists and talking low. Game planning. Behind me I heard Jim Glover's distinctive wheeze. Then, to the right, at the entrance to an open bedroom door, commotion drew my eye: a clipboard on the linoleum floor, a white Styrofoam cup sitting in a puddle, someone's crouched ass and shoulders filling the doorframe, another person beyond in the shadows, a third standing rigid just inside the door with a hand to her mouth. It looked like Rachael Uganavich, one of the nurses.

I couldn't quite see what was going on in there, but it was definitely the origin of the bird noises, which, now that I was at the interior of the unit where noises weren't so distorted and bent, I didn't think sounded much like a bird at all. Sounded exactly like what it was: someone— someone young—wailing in hitching hysterics.

Jared, a mid-twenties grad student with gold eyeglasses sliding down his sweaty face, pushed a pair of rubber gloves into my chest. "What's the deal?" I asked taking them without looking, my eyes still on the scene down the hall.

Jared pushed his glasses up his nose. "Lee," he said, as though no more details were necessary.

I turned to him now. Blinked. Waited for more. Jim snapped his gloves on. "Fuck," he sighed.

I blinked again, shouldered a track of sweat from my cheek. "What's that mean? Who's Lee?"

"Lee what's-his-face," Jim said. Now he was staring down the hall as well. "That new guy who came down here last week."

I knew who he was. Somehow, with that siren of a cry, I couldn't quite focus. More sweat tickled my neck like spider legs. Jared looked passed me, to the front door. "This it? Anyone else coming?"

Jim shrugged. "Lot of call-outs tonight." It was why I was doing a double. Night staff was too smart to come into this sweltering mess. Stressful enough on a cool night, but this hot? Counselors got tense, patients got edgy. The thermometers seemed to be measuring collective blood pressure. Recipe for a shit-show, just like this one, right on cue.

I pieced together that the cries were coming from one of the new hires, a girl straight out of undergrad, twenty-two. I'd seen her in the cafeteria escorting her small group. She looked even younger than that, a petite thing with a long brown ponytail and no makeup. Looked like a smart girl, a brainy type. Probably a psych major, thinking about social work one day, trying to pocket a little experience for the résumé. Probably lived in Brookline with a couple other girls, a futon for a sofa and a checklist on the fridge designating the chores. I'm not sure why I thought all that, but I did. I guess I've been seeing the type here for a long time now.

Jared mentioned that her name was Valerie, and on her round of checks she'd made the mistake of walking too far into Lee's room; you weren't supposed to let yourself get blocked in like that. Lee, who I guess was already pissed off about his doctor not making his appearance today to grant grounds privileges, cold-cocked her from behind, knelt on her back, and punched her two or three more times before abandoning her to storm off into the bathroom yelling the whole time not to mess with Mister Fucker. In fact, behind Valerie's crying, I could make out Lee's voice in the bathroom. Sounded to me like he was saying something like *mystify*, but I guess not. Mister *Fucker.*

"Stay in your rooms. We'll let you know when it's safe." Jim was making the quick rounds, reassuring patients who were sticking their faces through their open doors.

Jared waved us into a huddle, like he was about to call a football play. I felt uneasy letting this skinny shit strategize, but it was his unit tonight. We had five guys, which normally should have been enough, but Jim and I were really the only two with any kind of obvious strength and size. Jared was just a little puke. The other guy, Ben-Something, was in his sixties and took the overnight shift so he could write his novel or some such shit. I didn't know who the fifth guy was, but he looked nervous as hell. This was probably his first takedown.

Compounding this was the fact that Lee, from what little I knew, was a true maniac. I guess that sounds obvious given the fact that he was a patient in a locked-door psychiatric facility and had just beat the shit out of a 22 year-old girl, but I guess what I'm saying is that he was a maniac *in relation* to the others. Schizophrenic with

Narcissistic Personality Disorder. That was a real thing: Narcissistic Personality Disorder. Couldn't be reasoned with. Couldn't follow rules. Heard voices that told him strange shit. Couple hundred pounds of lean muscle. I guess the only weakness, our one advantage if we could exploit it when we went after him, was that he couldn't use his left hand because he had bitten his own fingers off.

I'd heard all this when he'd first been admitted. He'd been uncooperative, yelling, threatening to kill whoever tried to touch him. First time I'd seen him, sometime last week, he was sitting on a stool with wheels in the nurse's station not letting Nancy Kyle take his vital signs. I'd noticed the bandaged hand right away, how dirty it was, how odd it looked for reasons I didn't quite see until I was told later that under the bandage he was missing his pinky, ring, and middle fingers. He'd been at a family cookout over the Fourth, on a weekend pass from his group home, and, obviously in the throes of some psychotic state, squeezed a lit cherry bomb in his hand with his eyes squeezed shut and teeth gnashed while his nieces and nephews watched, forgetting the sizzling sparklers in their own hands. Doctors reattached all three fingers, which seemed crazy to me (wouldn't they have been blown to little bits?), and he'd been kept in restraints almost the entire time he'd been on the hospital's psych ward. A couple weeks later he was released to his family, and the very first night home he unwrapped the bandages, picked out the dried sutures, and then bit the partially-healed fingers off again, one at a time. His mother knew nothing of it until she got up in the middle of the night to pee and found the three fingers in the bathroom sink, large splotches of blood trailing on the floor all the way to his bedroom, where he was sleeping like a baby on a blood-drenched mattress.

***

"Mothafucks! Every last one of ya! Motha! Fucks!"

He was getting louder in the bathroom, even with the door closed. We walked by, not stopping, heading toward an unused bedroom. "We'll have to mattress him," Jared had told us, and we all seemed to agree, although, thinking about it, I wasn't sure of the logistics. Tough to mattress someone whose in a small bathroom. Too tight. Too many hard surfaces. Too much to go wrong. Still, he might have had a point—there weren't a lot of other options, not without someone possibly getting hurt.

From the empty bedroom Jim and Ben pulled up a plastic naked mattress. It was pretty thin, not heavy really at all. The idea behind *mattressing* was to enter a room with two people on either side of a vertical mattress, holding it there like an oversized shield. A few other people would be behind that, sort of the second wave of help. Ideally, you were supposed to walk in toward the patient, backing him (or her sometimes, but not very often) into a corner or against a wall, then press all your weight against the mattress, essentially pinning the patient to the wall. Then it was time for the second wave to come up on either side of this mattress/patient/wall sandwich and get a solid hold of each of his four limbs, maybe a fifth person to hold his head in one spot so he couldn't turn and spit. Once secured, the mattress was gradually let up on and the patient was pulled, quickly, to the ground.

They came back to the doorway, adjusting the unwieldy mattress. I had the leather restraints in a pillowcase hanging from my arm. "Okay," Jared started to say, his glasses slipping down his nose again. Suddenly the bathroom door banged against the tiled wall and there was Lee, right over Jared's left shoulder, big and sweaty and wild, with a shiny, rectangle toilet lid coming up over his head. I leaned back a step on sheer instinct before I knew what was happening, eyes fluttering in anticipation. I tried to articulate some kind of warning, but I think I just said, *"Hey!"* Jared flinched, still blind to what was going on but seeing our eyes train on something behind him, then hunched his shoulders in a half-hearted duck. Lee brought the toilet lid down and around in a wide roundhouse swing, laughing the whole way in strained grunts. I thought for sure in that moment that Jared was about to get his head knocked clean off, I really did, but somehow the lid almost seemed to go right through him, hitting the safety-glass window that looked into the dayroom. Glass erupted like confetti, dazzling in a strange, beautiful way. Thousands of icy chips plinked the floor, the toilet lid smashing into three clean pieces. There seemed to be this freeze-frame moment where nothing happened; Jared blinked, stunned, like he wasn't sure where he was. For some reason I didn't move right away either, looking from Jared to Lee and back to Jared, the weighted pillowcase swinging just above the sparkling floor. Lee jutted his jaw, his body stiff and puffed like a turkey trying to make a point.

But the frozen synapse of time cracked before it had even had time to register, and with a blur Jared dodged a flailing punch just as Jim scooped Lee into a headlock and yanked him backward to the floor. Jared tried to wrap up Lee's legs and went down too. Then more bodies, attempting to wrestle Lee's flailing limbs, swinging and kicking and lashing out, his body twisting atop what looked like a beach of diamonds. A wild knee triggered upward, catching Ben off the shoulder and knocking him back onto his ass. Finally I moved, crucial seconds too late, dropping the pillowcase and crouching to grab the loose leg, conscious of the floor. Without its laces, his sneaker— patients weren't allowed laces and often duct-taped their sneakers—came off in my hand. I tried again, reaching for his bare foot, falling forward onto my knees.

"I got his arms I got his arms grab that leg! Grab the leg!" I wasn't even sure who'd said it.

"Mmmpf! Fuck!" Not sure who'd said that either.

I fell forward, wrapping myself around the leg, pushing all my weight against him, like the rest of them were now doing. Holding tight and leaning, pushing down on him, pinning him. One of the female staff scurried past us toward the nurse's station. I could only see the lower part of her legs. Somewhere distant I could still hear the girl crying above all this, loud enough that I wondered if she realized the attack on her had even ended. Maybe she heard this ruckus, heard the yelling and swearing, and thought she was still on the wrong end of it.

Things slowed down. Lee couldn't move. None of us could really move, so focused on keeping him in place. Grunts. Heavy breathing. Almost sexual. All I could smell was sweat and B.O., so bitter I could taste it but too winded to close my mouth. I craned my neck to try to catch a glimpse of someone, read the next move. Tiny cubes of glass stuck to sweaty arms and necks and cheeks. We continued to quietly struggle for position, grinding ourselves into the glass but unable to help it. The linoleum was smudged red, ice chips pink with blood.

Lee snapped his head to the side and tried to hock a loogie toward us, but Jim, suddenly the fastest guy I'd ever seen, freed a hand and, stealing a fistful of hair at the back of Lee's head, pushed his face straight down into the chips and shifted some of his 300 pounds behind it. "No spitting," he told him.

***

Coming back into the unit on Ruth House, I was careful not to let the door slam. It closes by itself, and at two a.m. I was conscious of how loud it could be. You could sometimes feel the rattle in your teeth. The unit was quieter than I was used to, patients asleep, minimum overnight staff. Lights low. One of the counselors was in the common room watching TV with the volume soft, a clipboard on his lap, starting to slide down his thigh a little as he nodded off. From the nurse's station I could hear quiet voices, female. I wasn't quite as familiar with this crew. They'd changed shifts while I was gone.

I'd spent close to three hours at Grillo House. Once Lee had been controlled, we had to body bag him, always a long process. It's a way of transporting an out-of-control patient from one spot to another. Once bagged, the patient almost looks like he's rolled up in a carpet, his head exposed but supported, all other limbs wrapped tightly inside it. From there we lifted the bag by its canvas handles, four of us, and walked him to his room, then the long struggle to transfer him to the bed, leather straps binding him at four-points with padlocks, sweat dripping from our noses, running over our brows, backs sticky, the dead air sour. Rachael had come up behind Jared and pinched a gauze pad to his earlobe. It had been dripping like a leaky faucet since the toilet lid had grazed it. After, he drove himself to Faulkner Hospital for some stitches, and the girl, Valerie, went with him—her face swollen, purple and green, one eye closed. A slice near her eyebrow where her eyeglasses had crumpled. Made my stomach queasy. I wondered if she'd ever look the same, or *be* the same, for that matter.

I relieved Daphne of her one-on-one so she could squeeze in a quick nap. She'd been mandated to pull a double shift. Somehow, the hospital had the right to do that if they couldn't scrounge up enough coverage. I sat on the hard chair in the doorway to Eddie's room. Hurt to bend. The denim of my jeans rubbing the cuts on my knees. I'd gone into the bathroom and pulled my pants down back at

Grillo House. Fifteen or so little slices, all over, like little closed eyes, crusting with bloody tears. I stretched my legs straight out, crossed my feet, winced. Every muscle sore. I realized I was thirsty as hell, but it was too late; no one here to bring me a Dixie cup of water.

In the dark Eddie was snoring. They'd put him in restraints after I'd left. I pulled his chart onto my lap, my reading material for the next hour to try to stay awake. Said the staff couldn't get him to calm down, to stop flailing up and down the day room yelling strange things. They thought he was a danger to himself, to the others, too. I wasn't so sure he was a danger to anything, really. And the fact that he ultimately complied and let three staff, two women and one guy, escort him to his bed and allow them to two-point restrain him, left arm and right leg, with hardly a protest, sort of proved my point.

Eddie Fish's permanent residence was a group home. Like a lot of patients that landed on our doorstep, he'd gone off his meds and then gone off the deep end and become more than the group home's staff could manage. Not following basic rules, not checking in, missing curfew, yelling, making threats. So he got sent here, where he'd be safe and under a doctor's watch for a few weeks, get his medications straightened out. That was 80 or 90 percent of our patients. It was a short-term facility, sometimes as little as a few days or a week, maybe a month or five weeks at the longest. In a lot of ways Eddie wasn't anything special.

And yet I kind of liked him. Might have been his wild hair sticking out all over the place, or his laugh that crinkled his face like one of those shrunken apple head kits I used to have as a kid, that faded women's denim jacket a few sizes too small, the way he refused to wear a shirt underneath it. First time I'd seen him he'd been in the dayroom, standing by the window as if not quite accepting that he was caged in. The girl from the Activities Therap

Department was here, the one whose name I could never remember, and she'd brought her acoustic guitar like she did every Tuesday and Thursday at four o'clock. She sang and played while four or five patients sat around and listened. We encouraged them to attend, told them it looked good when the doctors read in their charts that they were socializing, helped them get grounds privileges and, ultimately, released earlier. So they sat politely and listened, some of them probably not even hearing her over their own inner voices. Eddie, though removed a little from the group, stood slouched with his long arms behind his back, looking out the window but smiling that crinkled smile and singing under his breath. Not just one song but all of them. Every single one. Every single word. Never blinking. "Fire and Rain." "Brown-Eyed Girl." Something else I recognized as Steve Miller Band. He even sang "The Do Run Run." Kind of. His lips, at least, were moving.

"John." His voice was hoarse, thick with sleep.

I looked up from his chart. A jolt of headache pain pulsed through the center of my brain, sneaking up on me. I'd never been so tired in my life. "Hey Eddie," I said, wincing.

"John, look what they did." He lifted his arm, the padlock banging against the rail. "Look what they did. *Tied me up...*"

"I see that. You gotta be quiet. Patients are all sleeping."

"Okay, John. Okay. I'll be quiet. I'll be so quiet." He'd picked his head up to look out at me, but now dropped it back to the mattress. "Laula's gonna kill me," he said. Then, "I gotta pee."

Laula. He'd meant Laura, his sister. I thought he'd said Claudia. I didn't know why. Every time he mentioned his sister I heard *Claudia.* My headache got worse.

His chart was thick. He'd been here three previous times. I'd read that he'd suffered a head injury in 1988, thrown from a flipped car. Never the same. Lived with his father for a while, who was off-and-on unemployed and battled alcoholism. The father passed away about ten years ago. For most of the last fifteen years Eddie had been in the care of his sister, and split time between living in her basement and living in group homes. He'd been in this last home for the past four years, since the sister moved to upstate New York when her husband was relocated for work. Said she wanted him to move out that way but the group thought he was finally acclimating well and learning some responsibility. The chart mentioned that he had a part-time job painting houses when there was work. He liked the concentration involved in painting. Said it kept the demons at bay.

"John, I need to pee. John."

I cleared my throat. "Okay." I put the binder on the floor and stood, my muscles tightening. Tomorrow I'd be immobile, I was sure of it. "Can you contract for safety, Eddie, or do I need to get you a bottle?"

I don't know why I talked like that. The lingo ingrained. *Contract for safety.* Why didn't I just say, *There's not going to be any problems, are there Eddie?* Why didn't I talk to him like a person?

Contract for safety.

"Yeah John. Yeah, contrasting for safely."

I was supposed to get the nurse, let her make the call. But it was after four in the morning, no one around. I pulled the keys from my pocket.

242

"Gotta really pee, John…"

"I know." I jangled the keys so he could hear them. "I'm coming."

***

I broke a second rule five minutes later, taking Eddie outside for a cigarette after he took the longest piss I'd ever heard in my life. Smoking hours ended at ten p.m., with the first of the day at seven. But Eddie was asking for one and I had nothing better to do. Poor son of a bitch stuck in those restraints, splayed on the mattress like a butterfly pinned down to a waxy corkboard in Biology class. I'd unlocked the cigarette locker and found his pack. Kool Lights, with a piece of masking tape wrapped around the front with *Eddie F.* printed in a Sharpie. I'd put two butts in his hand and stuck the lighter in my pocket.

Outside, Eddie sat on the bench he always sat on and sucked his cigarette, rocking forward and back, leaning his forearms on his knees, staring into the ground. The sky had the slightest hint of light to it, a muted grayness creeping in over the black. Looked like the sun was going to rise today. That was good.

Birds were awake. Christ did they get up early, squawking and chattering up a storm. Someone was standing on the front porch of Grillo House, a pinpoint ember tip of orange glowing then dulling, then glowing again. Someone smoking. Probably staff. What a night they'd had in there. Even the counselors who didn't smoke probably took a few drags tonight, steady the nerves. That motherless fuck Lee. That poor girl with the face. Their individual paths that had lead them, year by creeping year, toward this violent crossroad. The Ivy Leaguer with the family cottage on Martha's Vineyard, the theater group he'd been involved with, the passport in her jewelry box with stamps from Brazil, France, Belgium, maybe Morocco and Italy…

…and Lee, living on the streets, undiagnosed schizophrenia fucking with his brain all through his twenties, drug addict single mother, gave him up and sent him to *her* mother's, who was too old and too tired to do much with him. Let him quit school and bounce from shit job to shit job, getting arrested, drinking more, getting arrested again, then the psychotic break, maybe even a sexual assault that was never properly followed. A collision course leading the two of them here, Grillo House, August 8, 2012. You could almost call it destiny but it wasn't destiny at all. It was fucked up. A total fuck up, putting that girl in this situation. They took away Lee's pocketknife and neck chain and even his shoelaces, but let him pace the halls like a jaguar, letting the voices chant in his head louder and louder while a 22 year-old girl from a completely different world moved directly through his path like it was somehow, *somehow,* okay.

That wasn't fate, or destiny, or anything of the sort. That was just the wrong path, that's all it was. The fucking wrong path.

"I'm hungry."

Eddie smiled up at me, his small eyes red and irritated by the smoke. "What?"

I was actually surprised he'd heard me. Usually when he smoked he was impossible to reach. I finished taking in a long breath, almost cool in the pre-dawn. Almost. "I just said I was hungry, that's all."

He nodded, looked at me for a long moment. Smiled some more. Put the cigarette to his lips, his fingers shaking like they always were. "Hungry?"

I shrugged. "Yeah, a little bit." I watched a delivery truck grumble by in the distance, Roy Boy Breads. The street was hidden behind fences and trees and dense shrubbery. Or, I guess, the hospital was. "You wanna get some breakfast?"

The question hung there for a long time. Birds punctuated it over and over again. I wasn't even sure why I'd said it. I *was* hungry, that was true, but why had I *said* it? Eddie snickered at some kind of inside joke going on in his head, staring at a rock, the cigarette shrunken down to a nub, ash curling off it like a world-record fingernail.

Then, like a hiccup, I said it again: "Come on, let's get breakfast."

I didn't want to go back inside Ruth House. That was all there was to it. I felt it definitively, every ounce of resistance pulling away from it. The stuffy heat, the underlying smell of piss, the air of despair and pain and twisted, lost souls. I wasn't going back in. Eddie, I guess, was just collateral damage.

He put the cigarette out on the bottom of his flip flop and, pushing his hands into his deep cargo pockets, followed me to my pick up. We got in, wordless, pulling the doors shut and yanking the seatbelts. Eddie's visor was down and he looked at himself in the small mirror for a long time, a bemused grin of recognition peeling the corners of his face.

That girl Valerie wasn't the only one on the wrong path, I guess that's what had hit me. I was too, with this haunted house job and my sitting like a ghost outside my wife's place, watching my kids through the windows. I was too. And fuck it, so was Eddie. I didn't know what was going to happen after breakfast, whether I'd drop him off back here, or maybe take him to the train station and buy him a ticket to his sister's in Albany, or maybe just put a couple twenties in his hand and tell him go have fun for Christ's Sake. After that, it'd be my turn, whatever that meant. Right now, though, I wanted pancakes.

Eddie sat stiff, hands on his knobby knees, looking out the side window as the truck accelerated past Ruth House and toward the gates. His crazy hair danced like electricity with the wind coming through his window. "Go Fish," he said, either to me or, maybe, someone else entirely.

ABOUT THE AUTHORS

Delphine Boswell

Delphine's writing career began with freelancing and writing on assignment for such houses as St. Augsburg Press and Group Publishing, where her books for children were published. During this time, she had numerous articles for parents and materials for teachers accepted for publication. During the last twelve years, her writing interests have switched to fiction. She has had several short stories, in various genres, accepted for publication in EZines, print anthologies, and a literary journal. Currently, her newly completed novel *Unholy Secrets,* a noir mystery, is under consideration by an agent. Delphine quotes her passion for writing in the words of John Steinbeck, "I nearly always write, just as I nearly always breathe." In addition to her love of writing, Delphine has been teaching composition for almost twelve years to college students and presently teaches at Lake Tahoe Community College.

Alex Chase

Alex Chase is a university student who has had short fiction accepted for publication with Siren's Call Publication, Pink Pepper Press and Angelic Knight Press in genres including horror, romance and everything in between. When not doing school work, writing and exploring the depths of the human condition, he enjoys tutoring, working on his student paper, and running.

Facebook: www.facebook.com/alex.c.the.author
Twitter: @alexc_theauthor
Wordpress: theendlesschase.wordpress.com

Sean Conway

Prior to teaching, Sean Conway had spent several years as a mental health counselor at two locked-door psychiatric facilities in the Boston area. Later, he earned his MFA from the University of New Orleans as well as undergraduate and graduate degrees from UMass Lowell. His fiction has appeared in *Solstice: A Magazine of Diverse Voices, Glassworks, fwriction review, Digital Americana Magazine,* and other literary journals both print and online. He is a recipient of a Jack Kerouac Award, funded by the Kerouac estate, and most recently a Norman Mailer Center Fellowship. Currently he teaches writing and literature at the University of Massachusetts Lowell, and can be followed at www.seanconwaybooks.com.

Megan Dorei

Megan Dorei is a recent high school graduate who has just started delving into the publishing world. In October, one of her short stories- "Wings"- was published in Elektrik Milk Bath Press' *Zombies for a Cure* anthology. She is also currently scheduled to have four other stories published in various anthologies: "Haunt Me" in Less Than Three Press' *Kiss Me at Midnight* anthology, "Chasing Rabbits" in Sirens Call Publication's *Bellows of the Bone Box* anthology, "Half Jack" in Song Story Press' *Come to My Window* anthology, and "Love in a Laundromat" in Angelic Knight Press' *50 Shades of Decay* anthology. She lives in McLouth, Kansas with her family and the crazy friends who come to invade her house and steal her food.

Facebook: http://www.facebook.com/megan.dorei
Goodreads:
http://www.goodreads.com/user/show/14137016-megan

Aaron Garrison

A.A. Garrison is a twenty-nine-year-old man living in the mountains of North Carolina. His short fiction has appeared in dozens of zines and anthologies, as well as the *Pseudopod* webcast. His horror novel, *The End of Jack Cruz*, is available from Montag Press. He blogs at synchroshock.blogspot.com.

Connect with him on social media at:
www.facebook.com/aagarrisonwriter
www.twitter.com/@aagarrison1

Tom Howard

Tom Howard is a banking software analyst in Little Rock, Arkansas. He has published over twenty science fiction and fantasy short stories in the last two years, including sales to Andromeda Spaceways Inflight Magazine, Fear and Trembling, Resident Alien, Parabnormal, Epocalypse, and several issues of Crossed Genres. His writing is influenced and inspired by his four children and the Central Arkansas Speculative Fiction Writers' Group.

Russell Linton

In fourth grade, Russell Linton wrote down the incredibly vague goal of becoming a "writer and an artist" when he grew up. Taking a decidedly non-traditional route to this goal, he graduated from the University of Oklahoma with a Bachelor's in Philosophy and went on to a career in Graphic Design. Briefly sidelining those pursuits to be a Stay at Home Dad and for a stint in investigative work, he more recently returned to graphic design on a self-employed basis.

Throughout, Russell has continued to write collaborative fiction, ghost write for local business blogs and a few websites. However, his true passion is speculative fiction. His interests run the gamut from fantasy to science fiction and recently the dark paths of psychological horror. He has stories printed with Siren's Call Publications and online at Wily Writer's Podcast. Find him on his blog at www.russlinton.com.

Suzie Lockhart and Bruce Lockhart 2nd

After high school, Suzie Lockhart attended The Art Institute of Pittsburgh, but the gnawing urge to write always remained with her. Three years ago, she began working on an idea for a YA novel. When her son, Bruce realized he had the same passion for storytelling, they teamed up. Their joint efforts have produced short stories such as *Through the Looking Glass* in *Dionne's Anthology* *Arctic Weaver* in Sirens Call December eZine, and upcoming *Of Shadow & Substance* in *Sirens Call 'Mental Ward: Storie from the Asylum'*, as well as *Ten to Midnight* in an anthology from *Horrified Press*.

Suzie's first publication, *Instinct*, was in *DMD*'s *Frightmares, A Fistful of Flash Fiction Horror*. Another piece, *Be Careful What You Wish For*, appears in *Dark Moon Digest, issue #10*. She also has stories in the October and February *Sirens Call* eZines, and the March 1st issue of *Chicagoland Journal*. Suzie is delighted to be one of the female horror writer's to appear in *Mistresses of the Macabre*; look for *Playing with Fire*.

Bruce has a flash fiction story published in *Dark Eclipse*, Issue #7, entitled *Afflicted,* as well as *Signed, Sealed and Delivered* featured in *Dark Lore*. Upcoming, *Death's Final Request* will be in an August anthology entitled *Tales of the Undead-Suffer Eternal: Volume2*.

Both can be reached via e-mail at aspiringauthors2@gmail.com.

Jennifer Loring

Jennifer Loring has published nearly 30 short stories and poems in various webzines, magazines, and anthologies. She received an honorable mention in *The Year's Best Fantasy and Horror* for her short story "The Bombay Trash Service." Jennifer is currently studying for her MFA in Writing Popular Fiction from Seton Hill University. She is member of the Horror Writers Association and YALitChat.org, and works as an editor for Musa

Publishing's YA imprint, Euterpe. Jennifer currently lives in Philadelphia, PA with her boyfriend and two turtles.

Twitter: @JenniferTLoring
Facebook: https://www.facebook.com/JenniferTLoring
Blog: http://jenniferloring.wordpress.com

Sergio Palumbo

Sergio Palumbo is an Italian public servant who graduated from Law School working in the public real estate branch. He's published a Fantasy RolePlaying illustrated Manual, WarBlades, of more than 700 pages. Some of his works and short stories have been published in multiple publications, in both English and Italian, including American Aphelion Webzine, Alpha Aleph, Alpha Aleph Extra, Algenib, Oltre il Futuro, Nugae 2.0, SogniHorror, La Zona Morta, edizioni Lo Scudo, Antologia Robot ITA 0.1, Antologia Il Segreto dell'Universo, Antologia E-Heroes, WeirdYear Webzine, YesterYearFiction, AnotheRealm Magazine, Alien Skin Magazine, Orion's Child Science Fiction and Fantasy Magazine, Farther Stars Than These, on Digital Dragon Magazine, on Kalkion Science Fiction and Fantasy Web Magazine, Quantum Muse, Surprising Stories, EMG-ZINE, The Speculative Edge Magazine, Australian Antipodean SF, Schlock!Webzine , SQ Mag. Some of his short fiction can also been found in print anthologies from Sirens Call Publications, Schlock Magazine, by Chamberton Publishing, as well as soon to be released anthologies from Crushing Hearts Black Butterfl Publishing, Horrified Press, Sirens Call Publications, an Static Movement Publications.

Sergio is also a scale modeler who likes mostly Science Fiction and Real Space models; some of his little Dioramas have been featured in magazines and on websites. You can find some of his models online at his model clubs website at: www.lacenturia.it.

Joseph A. Pinto

Joseph A. Pinto is the horror author of two published books and numerous short stories; his most recent works can be found at Sirens Call Publications and Cruentus Libri Press. He is a member of the Horror Writers of America as well the founder of Pen of the Damned, a collective of angst and horror driven writers. Indulge in his unique voice on his personal blog josephpinto.wordpress.com and penofthedamned.com. You can follow him on Twitter @JosephAPinto. Joseph hails from New Jersey where he lives with his wife and young daughter.

D.M. Smith

D.M. Smith was a management consultant before quitting to study journalism and become a freelance writer. Her head still writes for the corporate world, while her heart is pulling her into creative writing. In another lifetime, she was once a biomedical scientist.

Printed in Great Britain
by Amazon

58424094R00149